Dear Reader,

I wrote *Love Bethany* for the hopeless romantics. The road to discovering love is not as straight and narrow as it has been in the past. Many of us have to learn hard lessons about self and life before receiving what we really desire. In the process, many of us give up on love, but there is a remnant of people who still believe in the power of love regardless of the unplanned detours.

My book is for:

Those who are still waiting on mister or misses right,

Those who fight to still believe in love,

Those who are on a self-discovery journey,

Those who wonder if love is a matter of choice than a divine appointment.

I am no expert in the field of love, but through writing this novel, I strive to provide a platform for conversations to be had that are secretly disturbing the faith of those who once believed that love always wins.

Sandreka Y. Brown

love bethany

BY SANDREKA Y. BROWN

iSeebookz Publishing
Lagrange, GA

LOVE BETHANY

ISBN:978-0-9995869-5-2

Cover & Book Design by Priscilla Sodeke

First Edition: April 2019

10 9 8 7 6 5 4 3 2 1

love bethany

prelude

THE PHONE RANG NUMEROUS times in her ear until a click sounded. Soon she heard, "You have reached the voicemail of... Please leave a message after the beep." She took a moment to breathe deeply, and then her voice trembled as she held back the tears. Never had Bethany thought she would have the guts to call and end her relationship with him... She believed in divine interventions and strongly believed "he" was God's way of righting the wrong that was done to her by ex-boyfriend Nick.

Bethany dated Nick for a whole year without knowing he was married. She met him at a time when she was fed up with being the "good girl." Her adult life had resulted to work and church as she watched others who weren't so dedicated to God get the blessings she desired. She learned, from many messages concerning single Christians, that in order to get a mate, one must first develop a relationship with God. Secondly, operate in his or her purpose, and then the mate will come. Bethany had been walking with God since the age of twelve, she discovered her purpose as a sophomore in college, and now she was a sexually frustrated mate-less thirty-five-year-old who had been celibate for eight years before meeting Nick. She rededicated her life to God after losing her virginity at eighteen, to her first college boyfriend, and she became sold out for God. *Where has this gotten me,* Bethany often contemplated before she decided that it was time for her to take her life into her own hands to get what she really wanted…a man.

While visiting her family back in her hometown one summer, she met the smooth-talking, sexy Nicolas Jordan. They hit it off quickly, and Bethany was determined to make him a keeper. She was finally experiencing the love she dreamt about. They were the epitome of long-distance relationships with frequent calls, every other weekend visits, vacations, and sex galore. It didn't even bother Bethany that he was a forty-two-year-old man living with a friend who was never home as he was a personal assistant to a CEO of a fortune 500 company. Nick told her that he was re-covering from his divorce, and she was okay with that.

She'd never forget their vacation to Miramar Beach Florida. Along the drive there, Bethany felt, exactly, what she was missing when she was trying to be Per-fect Patty. She had found the love of her dreams, but then she was abruptly awakened. Nick received a text on the drive, and after reading it he made a phone call. Bethany heard a woman on the other end. "No." Nick calmly replied to the call. "I'll let you know."

"Who was that?" Bethany could hardly wait for him to end the call.

"Business." He immediately responded.

Bethany didn't believe him, but she didn't want to start their vacation with arguing. She needed this time of relaxation.

The second day of their trip, Nick received another call from another woman.

"How's your training going?" The woman's voice from the phone said.

"It's going okay. Just some boring classes they got me taking. Can I talk to you a little later?"

"Sure."

Bethany's blood pressure started to spill over like boiling water, and she struggled to keep her cool.

"Who was that?" She asked as soon as he ended the call.

"My children's mother."

"What in the hell did she want and why does she think you are on a work trip? Is that the same woman that called yesterday?"

"I don't like people knowing my business."

"Are ya'll still messing around?"

Nick remained silent as Bethany ranted and raved on her unsure accusations. He didn't say another word. When Bethany finished her rant, she buried her tearful face in the bed. When the wimps from her crying faded, Nick slowly rolled Bethany to her back. "Stop," she said, but Nick unfastened her pants and pulled them off along with her panties. Soon she ceased saying stop as Nick's kisses, in all the right places, reminded her why she loved him so much. When he finished pleasing her, he kissed her forehead and whispered that he loved her.

After making sure Bethany was feeling much better, Nick jumped in the shower. Bethany continued to lay in the bed thinking about the events of the day. She knew if he was lying that it would soon come to light, so she decided to enjoy the rest of her trip.

Hearing her text message notification, Bethany rolled over to the nightstand to check her phone. Instead of grabbing her phone, she picked up Nick's wallet that he left open beside her phone. *Georgia! Why does he have a Georgia address?* Bethany grabbed her phone and took a picture. She never said a word to Nick about it, but she kept it until she felt like she needed to use it.

While visiting her mother on Mother's day, she could not reach Nick on the phone. She called and called as she desperately wanted to see him before heading back to Huntsville. Each time there was no answer. She hadn't heard from him since their Good Morning text. This was very strange, and Bethany's intuition lead her to believe that something fishy was going on. She knew this was the day she needed to find out where the Georgia address led to on his license.

"That son of …" Bethany called Ne'cole to vent her anger.

"Calm down Bethany," Ne'cole prayed that Bethany wouldn't do anything stupid like go ring the doorbell.

After arriving at the address, Bethany couldn't believe her eyes. There sat a beautiful brick home with Nick's truck, motorcycle, and the boat that she had seen at his friend's house. There also was a van in the yard with two little boys running in the grass and a beautiful Asian looking, short-haired woman standing in the door.

"I'm going over there!"

"Don't do that Beth." Ne'cole pleaded with Bethany. "You don't know that woman and how she will react."

"I don't care. I can't believe he's been lying to me. I hate him."

Soon she saw Nick standing behind the woman and kissed her before he walked out the door to get on his motorcycle. Nick's eyes looked like a deer in headlights as he saw Bethany's car parked in the empty lot across from the house.

"I'll call you back." Bethany hung up on Ne'cole. Ne'cole called back several times, but Bethany ignored the calls and followed Nick back to the Alabama line to his friend's house. She had every notion to run over him, while he was on his bike, but she loved him too much. Bethany jumped out the car as soon as she pulled into his friend's driveway.

"How could you do me like this?"

Nick remained silent as Bethany lashed out all of her anger.

"Are you finished?"

Bethany wiped the tears from her eyes and listened to what he had to say.

"Baby, I don't love her. I'm there for my kids."

"You lying Nick. I hate you."

Nick look annoyed, as he took a seat on the outside swing and Bethany sat on the hood of her car. She sat and called him every name in the book. Nick calmly ignored her and walked toward the backyard gate where he kept one of his bulldogs. Bethany sat quietly, as she contemplated what he was doing. She thought, *I know he isn't going to do what I am thinking.* As the gate opened, a bulldog came toward her. Nick looking surprised called the dog back, but the dog wouldn't listen. Bethany ran to the driver side door, and as she got in, she saw Nick trying to subdue the dog. They locked eyes, Nick looked concerned, but she thought she saw a smirk as she started her car and drove off.

From that moment she was done. It took Bethany almost a year to get over that hurt with her ex-boyfriend Nick... Prayer definitely became her outlet, and she felt as if God had answered her prayers and sent her a good Godly man with "him..."

chapter one

THE FIRST TIME SHE'D seen "him" at Saturday prayer service at City View Metropolitan Church, Huntsville's largest church, on a cool winter morning, she couldn't take her eyes off of "him."

He was neatly dressed in his khaki slacks and polo shirt with a pullover sweater, standing over 6 feet tall with his hands lifted in worship. Lord knows she did not go looking for a man, but he was pleasant to her eyes; tall, dark, and handsome to say the least. She tried to stay focused and pray but her prayers that morning surely was not the Lord's Prayer. Throughout the service, Bethany became distracted with thoughts of him, and again later with her best friend Ne'cole during their girls night out.

She could hardly wait to tell her about him, and how his very presence made her feel like she was in heaven.

The service ended, and later that day, Bethany and Ne'cole went to the local grocery store to buy popcorn and wine to go along with their movie.

"You've got to be kidding me," murmured Bethany as she saw him pushing his grocery cart down the bread aisle. "Girl, don't look now but that's the man I saw at church this morning, he is so fine to me."

After a quick moment passed, Ne'cole looked at the man. "Girl, yes! That's the kind of man you need right there. He's dressed nicely and looks professional. This is the one for you! Don't look now but he's coming this way. Be cool."

Bethany was a confident woman, but at that moment being dressed in her spandex yoga pants that accentuated the thickness of her hips, thighs, and buttocks that she deemed as both a blessing and a curse, she felt a little insecure.

Surely, he wouldn't be interested in me, she thought to herself. I'm probably too big for him. At times, Bethany struggled with being a size sixteen. More so, she absolutely hated her double D breasts which she perceived added an extra twenty pounds to her weight. Her secret insecurities continued to drip like a leaking faucet as she thought of other reasons he wouldn't be interested like the small gap she had between her front two teeth.

He nervously glanced at Bethany as he slowly pushed his cart.

Damn. Look at those curves. Damn! Look at those curves! He normally preferred a woman around a size twelve, but Bethany was packaging her weight nicely. *This must be God*, his thoughts shouted.

A nice churchman, was the thoughts swimming in Bethany's mind.

His current view of her appearance distracted his mind's process of how he would approach her. He had recognized her from prayer service that morning, and wanted to speak to her then, but he was too shy.

Now fate was giving him another opportunity, and he had a purpose to seize it. Looking at her face, he gazed at her smooth mocha skin that didn't have one spot or blemish. Getting even closer in proximity to Bethany, her eyes burst his thoughts like a needle popping a balloon.

Bethany, on the other hand, nervously lifted her eyes to see this tall, bald, and chocolate hunk of a man with a beautiful white smile looking right at her.

"Excuse me. Didn't I see you at City View Church this morning?" He asked curiously, speaking first.

"Hi. I was there. I thought you looked familiar. My name is Bethany."

"Nice to meet you, Bethany."

Ne'cole turned her back and laughed softly. "I like him," she whispered to Bethany.

"I'm sorry I didn't catch your name."

"Forgive me. I'm Caleb."

"It's nice meeting you as well, Caleb. Did you enjoy the prayer service this morning?"

"It was great. I love the worship songs played during prayer."

Ne'cole coughed, and Bethany realized that she had not introduced Ne'cole to Caleb.

"Please forgive my manners. Caleb, this is my friend Ne'cole. Ne'cole, this is Caleb."

Bethany watched as they greeted each other, and innocently Ne'cole smiled as if Bethany had not previously mentioned Caleb.

"I don't want to hold you ladies up from your shopping. I just wanted to speak to you," he said as his white teeth sparkled right into Bethany's eyes.

"Thank you for speaking Caleb."

They wished each other a good evening, and Bethany and Ne'cole continued their shopping mindlessly tossing chips, dip, cookies, and ice cream in their cart as they were too busy gabbing about Caleb.

"So, what you think girl?" Bethany excitedly asked her best friend for approval.

Calmingly, Ne'cole gave her approval. "He's handsome. Looks like he is a businessman, and he's in the church. Can't beat that girl."

"Do you think he is interested in me?"

"Girl, don't do that."

"Do what?" Bethany confusingly asked.

"Doubt yourself. You're a great catch."

"Yeah, I am."

"Bethany, it's your time. You deserve a good man."

"Girl, I might not even see him again."

"What will be-will be."

"Yeah. Plus, I need a Godly man."

"Because Nick sure wasn't," Ne'cole added.

"Honey he was Lucifer himself if you ask me."

They both laughed in agreement.

"Yeah, I'm trying to get my walk right with the Lord. Starting over at this new church has been just what I needed."

"Won't he do it!" Ne'cole charismatically blurted out.

"Yes, Lawd," Bethany replied as she lifted her hand and waved it from side to side.

"Anyways, what color will my maid of honor dress be?"

"Girl, you're silly. I don't know if he is the one yet."

"I can feel it, Beth. That's your husband."

"So, you're a prophet now?"

"Far from it child."

As they approached the checkout counter, Bethany's eyes suddenly went wide, and she grabbed Ne'cole's shoulder, quickly shaking it back and forth. "Honey!" Ne'cole said with an irritated look on her face. "You are going to pull my shoulder out of socket, Bethany! What is it?"

"Look! There he is again," Bethany said as she began to blush.

Caleb was checking out at register three, the same register they were headed to check out their items.

"You've got to talk to him again girl. I've never seen you like this. Go ahead."

Bethany moved to the front of their shopping cart and quickly turned to signal Ne'cole to hide the wine in their cart, unsure of Caleb's stance on alcohol. She did not want her chances to be ruined with him. Bethany only drank alcohol occasionally, and girls' night was one of those times.

"Hello again. I promise we're not following you."

"It's quite alright," Caleb said laughing as he unloaded his items onto the counter.

After the laughs faded away, Bethany seized the moment for even more conversation.

"So, what Sunday service at City View do you attend?"

"I attend the 9:30 service."

"What a coincidence! I attend that service too."

"Really!" Caleb's eyes widened with excitement.

"Yeah, I do. Maybe that's why I haven't run into you. There are over 20,000 members."

Caleb reached into his pocket and pulled out his business card to give to Bethany. She did not expect that from him and was not prepared to exchange cards with him. As a matter of fact, she didn't have business cards. Her face was emotionless yet filled with excitement like she was just cordially talking to him and not interested when he handed her his card.

"Call me anytime," Caleb invitingly said with a smile.

"I will."

"You ladies have a good night."

"You have a good night too," Bethany calmly replied.

Ne'cole lifted her head from unloading the cart and wished him a good night too.

As Caleb left the register, Bethany took a moment to exhale before she turned to look at Ne'cole, who was smiling and unloading the shopping cart.

"Why didn't I give him my number?" Bethany said frustratingly.

"No worries, girl. You are going to see him again. You did well."

"I certainly hope so," Bethany sadly murmured.

With a personal motive, Bethany suggested to Ne'cole that they end their much-needed girl time with Sunday service that next morning. Ashamedly, Bethany had disowned that worshipping God was not her primary reason for her wanting to go; instead, it was the possibility of seeing Caleb.

Service lasted about an hour as usual, and when it ended, Bethany and Ne'cole spotted him as they entered the foyer.

Never taking her eyes off him, Bethany uttered, "I'm going to speak to my future husband."

She was dressed to impress as she confidently walked toward him in her black wrap dress, black tights, blue jean jacket, and brown knee-high boots with a 4-inch heel. Ne'cole waited near the church's bookstore as Bethany approached Caleb.

"Excuse me. Caleb? Hello! I didn't think I would see you this morning."

Caleb's eyes lit up as if he had seen an angel. After he pulled himself back together, he finally responded.

"Hey! How are you? It's good to see you. You look very nice this morning."

"Thank you kindly. You're looking good yourself."

Bethany worried that she was smiling too hard, but as her eyes scanned Caleb's face, it was pretty clear that they were happy to see each other.

"What did you girls get into last night?"

"Oh! We just watched a couple of movies at Ne'cole's house."

"Nice!"

"Did you do anything special?"

"I got up with my boy, Antonio, and watched the Heat and Lakers game."

"The Heat won, right?"

"And you know this! Let's go Heat," Caleb said as he momentarily cheered for his favorite team.

"Sounds like you're really happy they won."

"Yeah, that's my team," he said with that bright white smile.

"How long have you been a member here?" Bethany asked, changing the subject to keep the conversation fresh.

"I actually haven't joined yet. I've been visiting for a few weeks now. What about you?"

"I'm not a member, either, but I plan to attend the class tonight for people who are interested in joining. You should come too."

Bethany looked at Caleb with a smile that she hoped would convince him to say yes.

"What time is the class?"

"It's at 6:00."

"Okay. I should be able to come."

"Great! I hope to see you later."

"That's the plan, Ms. Bethany. See you later."

Bethany arrived to class around a quarter to six, and she quickly spotted Caleb near the refreshment table getting a slice of strawberry cake and a bottle of water.

"Hey, you! I see you made it."

"Hey!" Caleb said, putting his plate and bottle down to hug Bethany.

Bethany could have melted in his arms. His scent screamed a familiar cologne, which happened to be her favorite scent on a man.

"I'm glad you could make it."

"Me too."

"Do you mind if I sit with you?"

"No, I don't mind at all."

Bethany had continued to ask more questions as she discreetly tried to get to know more about him.

"So, are you from Huntsville?"

"I am. Are you?"

"No, I'm originally from Auburn."

"Oh cool! War Eagle!"

"Actually I roll with the tide," Bethany smiled as she watched Caleb's eyes widened.

"I'm going to pray for you," Caleb whispered, as the facilitator welcomed everyone to the class.

The first activity was a questionnaire to help the parishioners discover his or her spiritual gifts.

Bethany and Caleb shared the same spiritual gift which was a pleasant surprise. Ever since she led campus ministry her senior year in college, she knew she had a pastor's heart. Once when she was teaching a lesson on relationships, she received the revelation that her future husband would be her ministry partner. Bethany believed that her life's mission was to care for God's people and that her future husband would have the same exact heart. Even though doubt settled in after many years of being single and she started taking matters in her own hand, deep down Bethany always wanted a man that shared her faith and her passion and service to God.

Caleb's eyes may have appeared to be on the facilitator, but he had his moments of glancing as well. Inwardly, he was more thrilled than Bethany, but his male pride kept him cool, calm and collected.

"So, did you enjoy the class?" Bethany turned and asked him after the dismissal.

"I did. Thanks for inviting me out."

"Yeah, I'm glad you came."

There was a moment of silent awkwardness as they both tried to ignore the elephant in the room.

"I guess I need to get going. I have an early start." Bethany hated the silence, and even though she wanted to talk to Caleb some more, she couldn't hold back her excitement any longer and needed to talk to Ne'cole.

"May I walk you to your car?"

"Sure."

Caleb walked Bethany to her car and gave her a sideways church hug to end the night. Bethany wished him a good night, and they parted ways.

chapter two

"YOU HAVE REACHED THE phone of Ne'cole Jones. I am unavailable at the moment. Please leave a detailed message, and I will return your call as soon as possible."

Bethany ended the call. Ne'cole was terrible about listening to her messages so, Bethany sent her a text instead.

> *Nikki!* Whenever she called Ne'cole that name, she was serious as a heart attack. *I believe he really is the one. I need to fill you in on the class tonight at church.*

Moments later, Ne'cole replied that she was helping Malik with his homework and asked if they could meet up for Margarita Monday tomorrow for some girl talk. She wanted to hear all about it, but mommy duty often made her unavailable.

Bethany arrived first as usual and got a table for the two of them. After twenty minutes of telling the waiter to come back, drinking ice water, stuffing her face with chips and salsa, and roaming through her Facebook feeds, Ne'cole finally made it.

"I'm sorry girl. Traffic was horrible, and I had to drop Malik off at basketball practice." Ne'cole rambled as she took off her leather jacket and scarf.

"It's cool chic." Bethany waved the waiter over, and they ordered their favorite, a frozen pomegranate margarita.

"So, what's going on with you and Caleb?"

"Girl, he came to the class last night smelling all good. I saw him in the foyer, and we chatted for a while and sat together during the class."

"What!"

"Yes, girl. We took a spiritual gift survey during class, and guess what?"

"Now Beth, you know I'm not good at guessing."

They both laughed in agreeance.

"Girl, we had the same spiritual gifts."

"That's good girl," Ne'cole calmly replied.

"Have you talked to him today?"

Ashamedly, Bethany bowed her head. "No, I haven't reached out to him yet, and I didn't give him my number."

"What are you waiting on?"

"Girl, I want the man to call me first."

"Beth, it's the twenty-first century. It's okay to call him first. Plus, the ball is in your court."

"I know," Bethany sighed. "What should I say? I don't want to seem desperate."

"Believe me he is waiting to hear from you."

"You think?"

"I saw how he was looking at you in the store and at church. That man wants to wife you."

"You so silly girl."

"Seriously, just pray about it. God will give you the words to say."

"You're right."

"Just don't call him tonight because you get a little crazy talking after margaritas."

"Whatever," Bethany laughingly raised her glass and cheered to having the best friend in the world.

Bethany often found herself smiling in a daze as she sat at her work desk two days after conversing with him that Sunday evening. She wondered if Caleb was thinking about her as much as she was thinking about him. Though she had his contact information, she was too nervous to call. She'd never called a man first. As the day progressed, thoughts of him only grew stronger. So, she decided to send him an email instead of calling.

Dear Caleb, I hope this email finds you doing well. I was thinking about you, and I just wanted to let you know it was a pleasure meeting you on Saturday and attending the class with you on Sunday. Hope you are having a great day!

Caleb immediately called his homeboy Reese, as Bethany's email popped up on his screen. Bethany had been on his mind ever since he saw her at Saturday morning prayer. It was something about her that he just couldn't shake. First thing Monday morning, he had to tell Reese about his weekend. Beyond her amazing thick physique, Caleb was in awe about the pastoral gift they both shared. He had felt bad about not getting Bethany's phone number before leaving the membership class on Sunday evening. Reese told him that she was going to reach out to him. He didn't believe it, and now his heart was leaping for joy.

"She emailed me," he told Reese over the phone.

"I told you she would." Reese didn't seem surprised at all.

"Yeah, you did." Caleb already was smitten by a woman he'd only known for a few days.

Bethany's nervousness diminished when Caleb responded in a matter of minutes. She wondered if he had been anxiously waiting for her to contact him.

Hey you! I was thinking about you too. It was a pleasure meeting you as well. How are you?

***

I'm good. I realized that I didn't give you my number the other day and I wanted you to have it. You can call me anytime.

***

Just saved it. I'll give you a call tonight.

***

Great! I look forward to hearing from you.

Bethany could not stay away from her phone for longer than two minutes. She came home immediately after work to wait on Caleb's call as if she was waiting on a check. She usually went for a walk at the nearby park each evening, but not today. She wanted to be available and undistracted.

What's taking him so long to call? she continuously thought as the clock struck seven o'clock. She decided to watch a movie to distract her thoughts. Not hardly five minutes into the movie, she fell asleep only to be awakened by the call she had been waiting for.

"Hello," she groggily answered the phone.

"Hey, did I catch you at a bad time?" His deep sexy voice perked her right up.

"Not at all. I dozed off watching a movie."

"I can call you back if you like."

"No, I'm good to talk. How was your day?"

"It was good. Been thinking about you."

"Oh really. What have you been thinking?"

"Just how amazing you are."

"You don't even know me."

"I know we have the same spiritual gift."

"Oh my god! So, you were looking at my paper?"

"Come on. Don't act like you didn't look at mine."

"Okay, I did."

They both bashfully let out a laugh.

"How do you like the church so far?" Bethany quickly changed the subject.

"I love it. I feel so much freedom than where I came from."

"Where were you a member before?"

"Greater Horizon."

"No way! I was a member there too."

Bethany and Caleb spent an hour just talking about mutual friends from their previous church and their good and bad experiences. Most of all, they both wondered why they never met each other before now.

"So, what do you have planned for tomorrow Beautiful?"

"Just work."

"Where do you work if you don't mind me asking?"

"I teach math at Huntsville Prep."

"School teacher, huh?"

"Yeah, I have been teaching for five years."

"I bet you are an amazing teacher too."

"Well, you know. What can I say?"

"Okay, Ms. JJ Evans. It takes a special person to be a teacher."

"You can do it."

"Oh no, I can't, I would probably have to lay my hands on somebody's child. I remember attending my niece's honors program because my brother couldn't attend, and the students were so disrespectful. I was so happy when the program was over."

Bethany laughed knowing just what he had experienced.

"Yeah, they can be. Some schools are better than others with behavior."

"It's a shame that ya'll have to deal with that and the parents."

"Yes, Lord! I could talk days on that subject, but I won't bore you. What's your occupation?"

"I'm an insurance agent at Zahlen Corp."

"Do you like it?"

"At times, I really want a job with the government."

"Cool. Do you have a college degree?"

"Yeah, I have a bachelor's degree in business. Did some missions to Africa and decided to concentrate on international marketing for my Master's degree."

"Nice. I'm sure that door will open for you."

"Thank you!"

"You're welcome."

"Hey, I know you have to get up early to teach the kids. I don't want to prevent you from your beauty rest. Maybe we can meet up tomorrow for coffee after work."

"Sorry, I don't drink coffee."

"Oh, I'm sorry."

"No need to be. You didn't know. How about a walk at the park near downtown around six thirty?"

"That's even better."

"Great! I really enjoyed talking with you."

"The pleasure has been all mine. Enjoy the rest of your night."

"You too. Good night."

Bethany sat holding her phone near her heart. She never believed in love at first sight, but she sure felt like she loved Caleb.

Bethany arrived first and waited for him by the swings. She had debated for hours on what to wear. Definitely not her work outfit. She didn't want to look like a teacher. She tried on a new pair of spandex workout pants, but she felt fat and didn't want to feel uncomfortable. She knew she wanted to wear black and kept digging through her closet until she found her fitted black joggers with the matching hooded top. *Perfect!* she thought before jumping in the shower to freshen up. She felt amazing as she took a final look at her Chinese bun, her evenly blended foundation, soft pink lip gloss, her silver medium size hoops, and her comfortable yet sexy joggers that still accentuated her most blessed body parts.

Even though she had seen Caleb before, butterflies filled her stomach as she watched him get out the car. He was dressed in an all black sweat suit looking like a fine tall dark piece of male chocolate.

Caleb looked calm on the outside, but his insides were raging like fire as Bethany was looking super sexy to him. It had been over a year and a half since he had been with a woman and Bethany's physique was causing Lazarus to be raised from the dead.

Bethany smiled and waved as she walked to meet him.

"Hello, Beautiful." Caleb reached out to hug her as he greeted her.

"Hey, Handsome. You smell good."

"Oh, thank you." Caleb played it off as if he didn't purposely spray his best cologne before getting out of the car.

"You look nice as always," he complimented as he grabbed her hand.

"Thank you." She managed to get out before her heart melted from his touch.

"Ready?" He asked as they started to walk around the pond in the middle of the park.

"Sure!"

"So, we never talked about age?" Bethany kicked the conversation off being very direct.

"How old do I look?"

"I don't like guessing," stealing Ne'cole's favorite line whenever she asks her to take a guess.

"C'mon. It's all fun."

"Uhm. Thirty-eight."

"Wow! That's a compliment. I'm actually forty."

"No way. You can't be."

"Yep. August 17th."

"Leo too I see."

"Wait. When is your birthday?"

"August 5th."

"What year?"

"19…1982."

"Wow, you are just a baby."

"I am a grown woman mister."

"I'm just saying I thought I smelled milk."

Bethany laughed at his comical jokes about her age, but she started to think about the decade difference they shared. Her parents were just ten years older than him.

"What are you thinking about?"

"Oh, nothing."

"Am I too old for you?"

"Not at all. I could use a mature man in my life."

"Are you calling me old?" Caleb asked as he began tickling Bethany around her waist.

"No," she said repeatedly through her laughter until he stopped.

"I am thirty-eight remember."

"Yeah, if you say so."

Caleb grabbed her hand again as they walked.

Bethany continued to ask her questions. "Do you have any kids?"

"I have a daughter she is 14. She lives in Africa with her mother, we speak often, and I have another daughter she is 10 and a son he is 8."

"Where are they?"

"They live with their mother in South Carolina."

Normally, Bethany did not prefer to date men with kids, but she didn't mind so much with Caleb.

"Does the baby have a baby?" He turned and smiled to ask her.

"No, this grown woman doesn't have a child."

"Really. You are rare. Not many women your age are childless."

"Do you want kids? Yeah, I want at least one."

"Any more kids for you?"

Caleb contemplated telling Bethany the truth. He didn't want any more children. He didn't want to be forty-something with a newborn. In spite of his true feelings, he told Bethany that he was open to it.

Changing the subject, Caleb asked her about her favorite genre of music. To his surprise, she loved old school 80's hip-hop and R&B. What did this young buck know about the '80s? The two discussed their favorite artists from New Edition to Prince.

Bethany also shared with him her love for basketball. She reminisced about the days her dad coached her. Caleb was an awful basketball player, but he was a huge fan. He found it pretty sexy that such a beautiful woman shared a great relationship with her father and was athletic. He never thought he would meet someone who met everything on his list. Maybe 80 percent, but not the entire list.

Bethany felt like she'd finally found her prince charming. Someone, who was a great listener. He listened to her talk about her students, her job, her dream of being a writer, and her spirituality without even complaining as they strolled through the park. Caleb took a deep interest in every word she spoke.

As the sun began to set, they continued to walk, and Caleb slowly took Bethany by the hand again. An unusual peace overcame her, and she moved a little closer to him. After a few more times around the pond, they headed for the parking lot.

"I enjoyed you," Caleb told Bethany.

"Same here. We have to do this again."

Caleb agreed and then leaned in to give her a hug that seemed to last for eternity. When he pulled back, they began to look each other in the eyes. He then placed his hand on her chin and slowly moved in and kissed her lips gently. Bethany wrapped her arms around his neck and fiercely returned his kiss.

Like a 4th of July fireworks show, Bethany did not want the kiss to end; so, she kissed him longer and was happy that she did. She was more persuaded that she had met the man of her dreams.

"I don't want this night to end," he whispered into her ear.

"Me either," she said resting her head on his chest.

"You wanna come over for a little while?"

"Well, I can for an hour or so."

Bethany followed Caleb to his apartment. She wanted to call Ne'cole, so badly, but she knew she would disapprove of her going over to his place so soon. All she kept saying over and over was do not sleep with him. After rededicating her life to God, she vowed to wait until marriage for sex.

"Excuse my place."

Bethany stood in Caleb's living room admiring how neat and clean he was.

"Your place is fine."

"Make yourself at home Baby." Caleb entered the kitchen and returned with two glasses of Moscato.

"How do you know I drink wine?" Bethany side-eyed him.

"I saw the bottle in your buggy at the grocery store."

"Oh really. Someone is pretty nosey."

"I would use the word observant."

"Same difference."

"Thank you," she uttered as she took the glass.

The glasses binged as they cheered to a new friendship.

"I have to be honest with you Bethany."

"What is it?"

"That kiss was amazing. Your lips are so soft."

"It was amazing. Where did you learn how to kiss like that?"

"Girl that was all you."

They both laughed as the magnetic waves were felt between their lips. Caleb leaned in and held her chin and started to kiss her again.

Bethany slowly leaned back until she was lying flat on the sofa, as Caleb kisses went from her lips to her breast. Bethany knew that playing around with fire could get her burned, but she was willing to play a little longer, as he began to take off her joggers.

His tongue was magical even if it wasn't in her mouth. He made her feel so good.

"You are so wet Baby."

Bethany was a little embarrassed about the river that was flowing from her well, but that didn't stop her from her closing eyes and enjoying the boat ride.

Suddenly she heard a wrapper opening. She opened her eyes to Caleb dressing his magic stick for intercourse. Bethany was not quite ready to go this far. She felt a little selfish after enjoying such a good oral performance, but she still didn't want to have intercourse.

"Baby, I'm not ready for that," she whispered.

"Okay." Caleb took off the condom and started kissing her again. Soon she felt a knock at her vagina door. "No Baby," she moaned.

Caleb said he wouldn't go in, but seconds later he lost control and begin to enter and exit abruptly through her vagina door.

Bethany just laid there thinking how she could enjoy yet hate the same thing at the same time. Her thoughts never became a mumbling word at least not to him.

chapter three

"BETHANY MONROE, WHAT HAVE you been up to?"

It had been a few days since she talked to Ne'cole, but she needed to update her about how things were going with Caleb.

"Nothing much girlie."

"You been up to something because you haven't been calling me. What's new with Caleb?"

"We met the other day at the park. It was so nice. We have so much in common. I really like him."

"You don't sound like it. What's wrong?"

"Oh, nothing. Just a little tired. I hung out with him late last night at his place."

"Omg! Did you…"

Ashamed to tell her bestie the truth, Bethany shouted no before Ne'cole could finish her question.

"I mean we kissed and played around, but no. It's too early for that."

t needs. It's okay. Just wrapped that thang

"Well, to be honest, I feel like he took advantage of the situation." Bethany busted into tears.

"Wait! What happened?"

Ne'cole waited until her crying slowed down to ask her again.

"Beth, what happened?"

"I mean I didn't want to have sex, but I did. Maybe I'm upset because I broke my vow to God."

"Have you talked to him?"

"No, I haven't."

"You should let him know how you feel. I have had that happen to me too. If you say stop, he gotta stop girl."

"I know."

"Look girlie. You know I am here for you. I'm walking into Malik's game. I am gonna to call you later."

"Okay."

"Love you."

"Love you too."

Bethany didn't see Caleb for a few days, but they texted nonstop. She had convinced herself that she wanted sex as much as he did. But she eventually explained to him how she felt about him going against her wishes, and he apologized.

Caleb invited her over for her absolute favorite dish, a sea broil, that Sunday after church. She mentioned the meal to her mother on the call before she made it over. Her mother insisted that this man was going to marry her.

Oh wow. How could she possibly know this? If my mother could sense it just from my conversations about him, this must be confirmation that he is the one for me.

For the next couple of months, they were inseparable. Bethany knew Caleb was in love with her. He had told her she was everything he wanted in a mate. He even showed her a list that he carried in his wallet of attributes and characteristics that he desired in a mate. She had to agree that she fitted all of his criteria. She was a Christian, loved to pray, was educated, had a good relationship with her father, and loved sports. He also had a secret love for teachers and seemed pleased that Bethany was one herself.

On the other hand, Caleb was her comforter. She would stop by his apartment many days after work, moan about her long day in his arms and then sleep for hours. When she stayed the night, she found it so attractive to wake up and see him praying early in the morning. She had always wanted a man like her father, who loved God, prayed, studied the Scriptures, hardworking, honest, and spoiled her mother.

Saturday morning prayer became their weekly ritual. No more having to beg a man to go to church. Bethany's heart was relieved with gratitude.

"Hey Bro! How are you?" Caleb spotted his homeboy Reese after the prayer session ended in the foyer.

The men greeted each together with a handshake and a hug.

The light complexion, medium size, average height man then turned to Bethany and introduced himself.

"Hi. I'm Reese."

"Bethany."

"Nice to meet you Bethany."

"Likewise."

Bethany looked at Caleb with a confident smile before leaving the two men alone to talk. It was just the excuse she needed to go freshen up in the bathroom; however, as she walked away, she overheard a truth that had been withheld.

"Bethany is nice bro!"

Caleb released a manly laugh in pride. "Yeah, she is."

"I can tell you like her."

"Is it that obvious bruh?"

"Boy, you are whipped. I can tell you like the young ones."

"Man, it's funny because she is more mature than other women her age and women my age."

"That's what's up! So, you know I got to ask."

"Anything."

"How's your divorce coming along?"

Bethany froze in her tracks as she overheard Reese's question to Caleb. She played things off as she had not heard anything, but her pot was boiling over inside.

"Hey Baby! Are you ready to go?" Bethany walked over and put her arm around Caleb.

"Alright bro! Good seeing you. Let's get up later. Pleasure meeting you Bethany."

"You too. Take care."

There was not a word spoken on the ride to Bethany's apartment. The guilt and fear of Caleb kept him quiet, and the calm before the storm didn't allow her to speak.

"Baby, I need to talk to you about something," he managed to get out upon arriving at Bethany's.

Bethany sat quietly dazing out of his windshield. "I have been separated from my children's mother for over a year. Our marriage is over. She moved to South Carolina with her new beau. There just isn't a divorce decree yet."

Tears ran down Bethany's face as she continued to keep her anger inside.

"Bethany, it is over between us. I don't even talk to her unless it is about our children. I'm sorry I didn't tell you before."

Bethany got out the car and slammed the door. She didn't want to hear any more. She got out without saying anything, but her tears communicated everything she was feeling at the moment.

Why in the world had he not told me he was still legally married? Bethany angrily thought to herself.

Bethany had called Ne'cole to tell her the news.

"Hey girl! You finally came up for air," Ne'cole jokingly said.

It had been about two weeks since they had talked.

"You won't believe what I have to tell you." Bethany sighed.

"What is it?"

"Caleb's married."

"No way! This can't be true."

Bethany told Ne'cole about his separation in detail.

"I'm sorry, Beth. What are you going to do?"

"I don't know. Girl, what is it about me that attract these married men?"

"It is not you. So many people are out here playing games. I can respect a man that tells me the truth and lets me decide if I want to be in that kind of relationship. Have you all talked about it?"

"No. He has been calling and texting me, but I told him I needed some time to think."

"Well, it's totally up to you, though, whether you continue things with him. No judgment here."

"What would you do?"

"Honestly, I would give him three months to take care of this situation. If he wants you, he'll get that divorce. Just talk to him about it. Hear him out."

Bethany pondered all of these things in her heart for the next couple of days, and even though she should have allowed Caleb the time to get himself together and keep her distance, he filled a void in her life. She felt heartbroken and needed a male companion, and he was just that to her and more.

Taking her best friend's advice, Bethany decided to call Caleb and share her thoughts. She took a moment to say a quick prayer and then proceeded to dial his number.

"Hey Baby. I'm glad you called me. I miss you."

"Listen, Caleb. I've been doing some thinking. I really like you a lot, but this situation does not sit well with me. I just came out of a relationship where I was badly hurt by a guy that lived two lives. He was married with a family."

Caleb sighed, "I'm not him, Bethany. I am not trying to hurt you."

"Well, why didn't you tell me this before?"

"I was afraid."

"Afraid of what?"

"Losing you."

His words penetrated her heart and Bethany took a few moments of silence thinking about how much she wanted him too. Confused on what to say next, Bethany thought about her earlier conversation with Ne'cole.

"Well, I am giving you three months and three months only to get a divorce."

"Really, Bethany! A divorce is not as simple as you think. It takes time and money."

"How much time? I have a friend that's a lawyer. I can give her a call."

"I don't know! Look, Baby, calm down. I love you and want to be with you. I can't promise you this will be taken care of in three months, but I promise it will be taken care of."

"How do I know you aren't lying to me?"

"Baby, you got to believe me. Just trust me. I'm going to make things right."

As hurt and confused as she was, Bethany continued to hang out with Caleb. She began to use him as a company-keeper both physically and sexually. She often told him that they were only friends even though she loved him. She was fragilely in love as she desperately hoped to not get burned by the situation.

Caleb was falling deeper and deeper in love with her. He was willing to do anything to keep Bethany in his life...even lie. He often accused her of taking things out on him because of Nick and not giving him a fair opportunity. Bethany fell for it every time and waited longer than she wanted for him to get his divorce.

Caleb did get divorced much to Bethany's approval, and she rejoiced with him as God's plan seemed to be back in effect. But her joy didn't last long as more of Caleb's secrets surfaced.

Following her ritual routine, Bethany stopped by Caleb's place after work. When she pulled up, she didn't see his car. She called him, and Caleb said he was inside. Bethany went up the flight of stairs to get to his apartment, and Caleb was waiting at the door for her. They hugged as she asked him where his car was. Caleb released a long sigh and began to tell her about his struggles to advance within the company and the cut throat practices he had to endure to make sales, and the backhand deals his colleagues made which reinforced his inability to consistently make commissions. So, he quit. He had been driving a company car, and after quitting he became car-less and jobless, which left him struggling financially and in danger of losing his apartment.

Caleb was a praying man, and soon his prayers landed him the job he truly desired with the federal government. Bethany was overly excited that Caleb was about to be back on his feet. He bought a used car, and it always broke down. So, Bethany became his personal taxi to and from work except he didn't pay a fare. Even after several paychecks, Caleb did not offer Bethany a penny unless it was dinner he cooked. Buying a car was always a discussion, but Caleb stated she didn't understand his financial vision.

Bethany struggled between walking away or standing by his side, despite feeling deceived. Perplexity grew within her with every passing moment. She was not experiencing the type of love she thought she had found. She found herself supporting him in ways that left her feeling empty. She wanted to go out on dates and take trips. This only happened if she financed the dates and she didn't quite feel like she thought a woman should feel while dating.

"Hello!" Bethany answered Ne'cole's call on the first ring.

"What's wrong Beth? You sound sad."

Bethany stayed silent for a few seconds until her tears started talking for her.

"Bethany! What's going on?"

Bethany continued crying as if someone had died.

"Bethany, I'm coming over. I'll be there in a few minutes."

Bethany and Ne'cole only lived half a mile away from each other. It was good to have her bestie so close. They had always been there to help each other pick up the pieces when life fell apart. Thicker than thieves was how most people described them. Bethany and Ne'cole were non-judgmental, and they allowed each other to live their life.

Ne'cole knew Bethany was a crier, but she rarely heard her cry like this since breaking up with Nick.

Ten minutes later, Ne'cole arrived at Bethany's apartment.

After several knocks and no answer, Ne'cole used the key that Bethany gave her in case of an emergency to unlock the door.

"Beth, it's me. I'm coming in."

Bethany's place was completely dark. Ne'cole carefully walked to the light switch tripping over an empty bottle of wine.

"Beth, are you here?"

She proceeded down the hall to the bedroom. Bethany was lying on her back with the covers over her face so still as if she was in a casket.

"Beth, talk to me. What's going on? Is it Caleb?"

Bethany sat up in the middle of the bed with both of legs propped up and buried her face in between. Finally, words began to form.

"Why does dating have to be so complicated?"

"What do you mean? Are you and Caleb still together?"

"I'm so tired Nikki."

Ne'cole knew this was a serious matter. Bethany rarely called her Nikki. Maybe Necy as her sorority sisters called her.

"I'm listening, girl tell me what's going on?"

"Caleb quit his job a while back. The car he was driving was a company car. He doesn't have a reliable car. For the last two months, I have been his ride to his new job, and he hasn't offered me any gas money. He said he was saving up to buy a car with cash because his credit was poor, and he got denied. We don't go on dates unless I pay. The sex is good, but Nikki, that's not enough for me."

"You love him don't you?"

"I do, and I care about him a lot."

"Well, you know I ain't the one to quote scripture, but doesn't the Bible say that the blessings of God addeth no sorrow."

"Proverbs 10:22."

"That's it, and girl, you seem sorrowful."

"I know, but he has a lot of potential."

"Girl, a man has to bring something to the table for me. I don't think a man should date if he can't provide for himself. How can he provide for a family?"

"You're right girl."

"Did you say that he doesn't give you gas money?"

"Yeah."

"What the hell? Naw Sis. He got to go."

"I know, but I believe his intentions with me are good."

"Bump that. You can't use intentions to buy gas."

Bethany knew everything Ne'cole said was true, but how could she let him go when she didn't want too. She had gained the company of a male, consistent sex, and great conversation, but she had become tired of playing the role of both the man and woman in the relationship. Nonetheless, the flesh was talking louder than her spirit, and she decided to hold on a little while longer.

On a portentous day when they'd had one argument too many, Bethany reached her breaking point. The name calling and accusations vexed her spirit, especially when Caleb reneged in anger of his promise to pay for her moving expenses to a new apartment near downtown Huntsville, closer to her job. He wanted to show his appreciation for all Bethany had done for him, but that was it. Bethany had vowed she couldn't take any more after he called her an adulterer. Caleb knew exactly how to break her down…with the Word. He often used scriptures in their arguments, and she felt condemned even though he was just as guilty. His antics had gone too far this time and Bethany had had enough. From that moment on, she didn't speak to him for seven months.

chapter four

ON VALENTINE'S DAY WHILE hanging with her new beau, Rasheed, Bethany got a text from Caleb.

> *Bethany, I hope you are doing well. I just wanted you to know that I am thinking about you. I love you. Happy Valentine's Day!*

"Who is that?" Rasheed curiously asked. "The past," she replied as she laid her phone beside her and crawled on top of Rasheed and kissed him passionately.

Caleb was a thing of the past, and she wanted Rasheed to know he had all of her heart. Well, at least he had it while they were together. It didn't take long after their relationship ended for her heart to long for the love she had with Caleb, but guilt kept her from reaching out since she ignored his Valentine's text.

During one of her Sunday church visits, Pastor Carlton ended his message, and Bethany's eyes widened in awe as the pastor called Minister Mitchell to come forth. It had been almost a year and so much had changed with her.

She was physically twenty pounds lighter and finally got the gap between her front two teeth closed with bonding. Her smile was whiter and brighter.

She started attending the Midtown campus of City View with her friend Brittany, after befriending her in a small group and hadn't seen Caleb at church. She'd never thought she would see him at this location but was glad she did. Bethany watched as Caleb walked past Pastor Carlton, and called the prayer team to come. She had always loved his commitment to prayer; it was one of the things that made him even more attractive when she saw him the first time.

She anxiously sat as the congregants cleared the sanctuary. Most of the prayer team had finished special prayer except Caleb. Bethany made her way down the aisle as soon as she heard Amen. Without any hesitation, Bethany greeted Caleb with the biggest smile. His eyes lit up when he saw Bethany walk down the aisle toward him. All of the anger he felt melted like ice cream in the sun as the love he had for her overflowed in his heart. He had loved Bethany from the very first time he laid eyes on her.

"Caleb Mitchell or should I say, Minister Mitchell. It has been a long time. How are you?" Bethany gave him the biggest hug.

"Hey, Bethany. How are you?"

"I'm okay. It's good to see you. I didn't know you attended this campus."

"Yeah, I moved to Midtown, and this was closer for me. I didn't know you attended this service either."

Caleb was in a much better place financially and had moved into another apartment and bought another car.

"I do. I started coming with my friend Brittany from my small group. She is out of town this Sunday, so I came to a later service."

"That's good."

"How have you been, how is Mama Hazel?"

"Mama Hazel is with the Lord." Caleb buried his mother months ago and held a dislike in his heart that Bethany was not there for him and it reminded him of his mother's non-nurturing spirit.

"What! Caleb, I'm so sorry. How did she die?"

"She had a heart attack."

"I hate to hear that. Why didn't you tell me?"

"Honestly, I thought you knew."

"No, I didn't know. I am so sorry. I loved your mother."

"I know. Mama Hazel loved you too."

"I feel so bad. I would have been there for you."

"Why didn't you call me?"

"I thought Ava told you."

"I haven't talked to Ava since I started attending this campus. She is the prayer leader at the main City View campus, and I haven't even seen her."

"Oh. That's strange. I just knew she told you."

"How is your dad and Aunt Cora taking it?"

"My father, he is dealing with it, but my mother's sister Cora had a stroke."

Bethany couldn't move, but her tears move rapidly down her face.

"Caleb, I don't believe this. How? When?"

"Aunt Cora had a stroke just a month after Mama passing."

"I'm sorry Caleb. I wish I would have known. I would have been there for you."

Full of guilt, Bethany apologized over and over for not being there for him. She wanted to desperately make things right and invited Caleb to Sunday dinner at the new Brazilian restaurant in town. Caleb never denied Bethany of seeing him and quickly replied yes.

How can you hate the person you love? Caleb's raging internal thoughts screamed. Bethany was everything he wanted in a wife. Smart, Spiritual, and she has a great relationship with her family. She was a classic lady in the streets and his freak in the sheets. Even being madly in love with her, he could not shake the fact that she left him like his ex-wife Tonya.

Caleb and Tonya were married for ten years, and two children were conceived. They had a handsome, well-behaved son and a beautiful daughter. Five years into the marriage, Tonya became pregnant with a set of twins that she secretly aborted. Caleb never told Tonya that he knew, and grieved less when he found out he was not their father.

Although Tonya supported him in many of his business adventures she wanted more and found a more financially secure man when his investments crumbled. He found out that Tonya often lied to him about her weekend girls' trip.

Tonya decided to officially take the children and herself to South Carolina where she thought the grass was greener after Caleb found out the truth. Tonya was the second woman he felt like didn't want him. Bethany's action made a third as his relationship with his mother was strained. He thanked God for Aunt Cora, and he had placed a level of hope into Bethany.

He watched Bethany as they walked, and he calmed his inner thoughts to enjoy the moment. They entered into a nearly crowded restaurant where they spent over an hour catching up.

"How are you really doing?" Bethany curiously asked after getting over the initial shock of the news that Caleb's mother had passed.

"I miss my mother. Some days I hurt. Ava and the prayer team really supported me during my mother's

47

passing and continue to be a source of support with my Aunt."

"That's good. We attend a really good church."

"Yeah, so what's new with you?"

"Well, I met a guy a few months back. Things took off extremely fast. He went with me to my sister's graduation and met my parents. Everyone loved him, but he was too much about self. Things just didn't work out."

"Oh, that explains a lot."

"I'm confused."

"I texted you on Valentine's Day and never heard back from you. I was deeply hurt and angry at you during that time."

"I apologize Caleb. I wasn't quite myself at the time."

Bethany was twisting the knife already in his heart with her words. She let a man she barely knew meet her parents. That was something he always wanted to do but never did.

"Bethany, I needed you there for me. No matter who tried to comfort me, it just wasn't the same."

"I didn't know! I'm here now. Will you allow me to be here for you now?"

Bethany grabbed his hands and leaned in from across the table and kissed him on the lips.

"Please Baby," she whispered.

"I think we should just be friends."

He truly meant friends with benefits. They became even more inseparable than before. Caleb held grudges against Bethany for leaving him. He was upset about the relationship she had with Rasheed. Most of all, he was angry with her for not being there during his time of sorrow. With a mixture of anger and love, Caleb let it all out in the bedroom. The connection they had in the bedroom became magical, and their bond intimately grew stronger.

After months with the relationship status of it's complicated, Bethany poured out her heart to Caleb as he walked her to her car after a special Wednesday night service.

"Caleb, I know that you are my husband. I know without a shadow of a doubt that God created you for me. I was wrong for not being there. I was wrong for leaving you. I love you so much."

"Wow! After all this time, you finally wake up. You didn't want me when I didn't have anything. You just couldn't wait for me to get things together. Well, things don't revolve around you, Bethany."

"So, are you saying that you don't love me?"

"All I am saying is that you will not rush me."

It had been two years since that day, two years of repeated cycles of love, sex, arguments, lies, dating other people, and reconnecting over and over again.

The last reconnection happened nearly four months ago when Bethany was preparing to release her first novel, finally fulfilling her dream of becoming an author. Prior to then, she had not spoken to Caleb in nearly six months.

Sitting on her balcony one summer evening in June, listening to sounds of singer Lauryn Hill and drinking a cold glass of lemonade, Bethany began to think about Caleb and how she'd used to read her writings to him before she was published. Her thoughts about him were so strong, to distract herself, she grabbed her purse and keys and went down to the local bookstore. She purchased a drink from the café and began to work on some final touches to her manuscript. It wasn't nearly an hour after she had arrived when the realization that her plan to distract herself from thinking about Caleb hadn't worked.

She had heard from Antonio, Caleb's best friend that he had moved to Metro-Atlanta with his girlfriend, Kacey after his father passed away. Bethany did not want to cause problems with his relationship. However, at the least, she wanted to send her condolences, to thank him for being a listening ear and to update him on the success of her book. Maybe this was the reason she was thinking about him so much. Although she was angry when she found out he had moved without telling her, she thought she would find closure by telling him "thank you", and maybe the thoughts of him would leave.

Since she deleted Caleb's number after their last break-up, Bethany chose to email him instead of asking Antonio for his number. Coincidently, this was how she'd first contacted him after they'd met.

Dear Caleb, I hope this email finds you doing well, So sorry to hear about your father. Would you give me a call? I only need two minutes of your time. Please and thank you!

Two hours later, Caleb emailed her back.

Can I call you tomorrow?

Around 3:30 the next day, Bethany started to breathe heavily, as she saw Caleb's number appear on her cell phone screen. She answered with a squeaky, "Hello?"

Calmness soon swept over her after hearing how excited Caleb sounded to be speaking with her. After the usual formalities and discussing how he was doing with his father passing, Bethany told Caleb that she really wanted the opportunity to tell him thank you and to update him on her book's progress.

"Bethany, I am so proud of you. I've been following your success on social media."

"Really?"

"Yes, I wanted to reach out to you, but I thought you had moved on. You looked so happy."

Bethany was not ready for what came next.

"Bethany, it's not by happenstance that you reached out; you've been strongly on my mind lately. I came home from church, a couple of days ago, and I literally fell on my knees. I told God to take away my thoughts of you or make a way for us to be together."

"No way!" Bethany said, not wanting to admit that she was happy to know that.

"I'm not lying to you. I never stop thinking about you."

They spent the next hour on the phone apologizing, sharing updates, and laughing about the good ole days.

Numerous calls and texts continued for the next two days. Once again, Bethany found herself enjoying reconnecting to the man she loved, but she could not deny the fact that he still had a girlfriend. One afternoon when Caleb called her after leaving work, she began to question him about the direction in which they were going. She explained with tears streaming down her face how she did not want to go through this cycle again. She told him if they were not moving toward a committed relationship, then she needed to end things now.

Bethany had heard the sadness in Caleb's tone. He mentioned that he felt like God had brought back his true love. He tried to reassure Bethany of his love for her and told her that he needed some time to figure things out.

Bethany pleaded with him to tell her the truth. Was he really going to leave Kacey?

"I'm not going to lose you again, Bethany," he'd responded confidently, indirectly answering her question. "I need you."

Bethany gave into the vulnerability of his voice, and they continued the calls and texts. She expressed to him that she was contemplating moving to Georgia to be a little closer to her family. Living the single life was getting hard for her, and she was getting homesick in Huntsville. Especially since Ne'cole had finished her doctorate in medicine and started practicing in another state, things were just not the same for her anymore. Caleb told her about two counties south of Atlanta, Coweta County and Fayette County. Plus, Caleb always talked about them moving to Metro-Atlanta together, and things were lining up from all the previous dreams to come to reality.

Bethany started the job search and applied for the two school districts suggested by Caleb. Within a week she had a scheduled interview. Boy did Caleb get excited. This would be their first time seeing each other since reconnecting. Bethany agreed to meet him after he got off work. She filled her time after the interview with apartment searching for the two of them.

Bethany watched the clock as she waited for Caleb to arrive at a nearby mall. She was anxious to see if there was still chemistry between them. It didn't take long after his arrival for her question to be answered. These lovebirds were smitten. The bond was stronger than it had ever been.

Bethany began to sweat in her pants as she became hot just being in his presence.

"Get out the car Baby and give me a hug."

Bethany got out and hugged him. Chills went down her spine because of his embrace, and within seconds the two lovers stood intimately exchanging kisses. Eventually, their lips departed, but they didn't want to let the embrace go. Absence really made their hearts fonder.

"Are you hungry Babe?" Caleb asked as he pecked her lips over and over.

"Yes, Babe."

"What do you have a taste for?"

"You."

They both laughed at her silliness. Bethany could be quite the comical flirt at times.

"You can have all of me."

Bethany didn't want anything heavy to eat, so that went around the corner to a fast food chicken restaurant.

"So, tell me about the interview."

Bethany let out a long sigh. "I don't think it went so well. It wasn't even for the position on the website. I was thrown for a loop with the questions."

"Really? I know you still did well."

"We shall see. The principal said she needed to call my references and it would be a few weeks before making a decision."

"Gotcha."

"But Baby, I looked at an amazing apartment for us today. It is a little pricey. What's our budget?"

"Tell me what you liked about it."

"Here is the brochure. It was a one bedroom, but it had two closets. That is perfect for us."

"You must like this place, huh?"

"I do, but it all depends on this job though."

"Would it be too far from your job?"

"It wouldn't be too far."

"Great."

Bethany got quiet when Caleb's phone started ringing.

"Hello."

Bethany heard the woman's voice on the other end. She knew it was Kacey when she heard her asked was he coming home before hanging out in the city.

"I'll be home a little later."

Bethany's blood pressure rose, and the obvious truth hit her right in her face. She sat across from him holding back the tears until he asked was she okay. Bethany sat in their booth and cried.

"You haven't told her yet."

"Baby, if I tell her now, she will kick me out, and I will have no place to go."

"Caleb, are you really going to break things off with her?"

"I'm not losing you again baby. I'm going to tell her, but I know this is going to hurt her."

"But what about me? What about hurting me?"

"Baby, this is not an easy situation, but I am going to tell her. Just give me a little time."

Caleb leaned over and wiped the tears from her eyes.

"I love you, Bethany."

Bethany managed to say I love you back, and she reached for a tissue to blow her nose from the congestion caused by her tears.

Caleb took Bethany back to her car. Saying goodbye was harder than fastening a pair of too-tight jeans, but it was getting late, and Bethany needed to drive an hour to get to her god-sister's house and get up early to head back to Huntsville.

Bethany and Caleb texted the whole night, and Caleb reassured her that God had everything under control. Bethany asked him if he thought it was God's will for them to be together. He knew without a doubt that God was working things out. He mentioned in conversation that he had to forgive Bethany for not being there when his parents died. That was stopping him from loving her in the past. Kacey was a good woman just not my wife he told her a few times. He prayed over and over for God to remove thoughts of Bethany out of his heart or make a way for them to be together and he was surely in the answering prayer business.

Bethany found comfort in his words and played them over and over in her mind on her return trip. As she pulled out her phone to let Caleb know that she had made it back to Huntsville safely, a call interrupted her text.

"Hello."

"Hello, this is Mike Nealey, the principal at Rising Star Middle School. May I speak with Bethany Monroe."

"This is she."

"Hi. I was calling to see if you would like to interview for a math position at our school tomorrow at 2."

"Sure. I just literally made it back from Newnan a few minutes ago, but I can make that work."

"Are you sure? I know that is a quick turn around."

"Yes, it's fine."

"Great! See you then."

Bethany's excitement outweighed the tiredness from driving and the thoughts that were working overtime about her and Caleb. She immediately texted Caleb with the good news. Immediately after her text, he called.

"Hey Babe. I thought you were working."

"I just had to call you after your text. That's great Baby. When are you leaving out?"

"I'm going to leave out around eleven tomorrow morning."

"Baby, this is a little further from your job."

"It's okay. I've wanted to work over at the south office that way anyway. I really want that job."

"For real?"

"Yeah, I'll start my application tonight."

"Cool."

"Are you gonna stay the night here tomorrow?"

"I wish, but I need to get back to work after taking two days off. I wish I had time to look for an apartment while there."

"Just pick up an apartment guidebook from a convenient store, and I'll get one too."

"I will."

"Get some rest Baby. I don't want you on the road tired."

"Yeah, I am about to call it a night."

"Let me know when you leave out tomorrow and how the interview goes."

"I will Babe."

"Bethany!"

"Yes, Babe."

"I love you."

"I love you too Caleb."

Despite being tired, Bethany drove back to Newnan. She had an amazing interview with Principal Nealy. She called Caleb as soon as she left the interview and talked him through it explicitly.

"Baby, you got this." He confidently knew that by the sounds of it this was Bethany's job.

chapter five

JUST A WEEK LATER, Bethany was offered a job at Rising Star, and she only had a week before starting. Since she could not find an apartment in such a short amount of time, her god-sister Lisel agreed to allow her to stay with her until she found one. She was now only an hour from Caleb, and things were finally panning out for them to be together. Bethany was thrilled to see Caleb's excitement in having her close to him. The long-distance phones calls were now frequent trips to a local bread and breakfast ran by an elderly couple who immigrated to America in the 1950s from Czechoslovakia. They were happy to see her and Caleb. They stated it was good to see young people committed and in love.

Bethany knew the B & B trips only ended with Caleb returning to Kacey. But thoughts of Caleb's girlfriend washed out each time she was safely embraced in Caleb's arms. They pleased each other naturally and fought past any guilt when it came to sex with each other. He confided to her that no woman had a touch that affected him the way hers did. He described it as healing to his body, and he craved sexual healing very frequently.

61

Honestly, Caleb pleased her too Bethany had to admit. It was like being in heaven while being intimate with him. She loved his versatility in the bedroom. He could be as gentle as a dove and take her on an exotic rollercoaster ride. They were perfect for each other. But deep down the truth still remained, he hadn't broken things off with Kacey yet.

Bethany had deeply believed that moving to Newnan would solidify all the plans and conversations that were happening on a daily basis with Caleb. She informed her parents about her move and the serious direction her relationship with Caleb had taken. Her parents didn't know much about him, but if he was making her happy, they were happy as well. Her younger sister, Jonee, was the most excited as she felt like the answer to her prayer had finally come. Bethany wanted desperately to be married but had not experienced a successful relationship and singleness had become her way of life. Bethany often talked to Jonee about how lonely she got living by herself. She told her to get a dog, but Bethany didn't like dogs ever since one chased her down the street in front of Nanny's house when they were kids. Their play cousin, Marlon, had to go get her from Mr. Jackson's screened-in porch. Jonee teased that fear made Bethany run faster than the speed of light that day. Jo, as Bethany would sometimes call her sister, told her to find a new hobby. She started learning how to play tennis. She could tell she loved it. Her face lit up like a kid in the candy store whenever she talked to her sister about her practices. She hoped maybe it was her coach, but she said it was a woman anyways. It was just great to see her big sis enjoying a little bit of happiness.

***

"Hey, Babe. I talked with my parents and sister tonight."

"That's great. How are they doing?"

"They are good. I told them about my move to Newnan and that you were looking forward to meeting them."

"Oh really?"

"Yes. That was okay, right?"

"Yeah. I thought you had already told them."

"Nah, I wanted to make sure we were serious. My dad seemed very excited. I told him that he didn't have to help me move because you were helping me."

"That's cool Baby."

"When will your apartment be ready again?"

"In about a month."

Bethany commuted to work for weeks waiting on her apartment to be ready. Caleb told her to pick what she wanted. He was still waiting to hear back from the request to transfer to the south office.

"Will you be moving in when I move in?"

"That's an hour one way to get to my job."

"But Baby we would be together. Wouldn't that make you happy?"

"I'm not about to drive two hours every day to get to and from work. I might as well stayed in Huntsville for that."

"An hour is the average commute in Metro-Atlanta Babe."

"I'm not driving an hour to work for no damn body."

"I would do it for you."

"No hell you wouldn't, and I wouldn't want you too."

"Why are you so upset Babe?"

"Why are you rushing things? I haven't heard anything from the transfer request yet?"

"Does she know you made the request?"

"No."

"When are you going to tell her?"

"Why are you rushing me to leave a woman who had been there for me during one of the lowest times of my life?"

Caleb began to tell her that she was trying to have things her way and in her timing. For a while, Bethany guiltily accepted Caleb's viewpoint as the truth and continued her limited relationship with him. But he began to sense her emotional distance from him with the reduced text messages and calls. Finally, Caleb could not hold back the truth he was keeping from Bethany any longer.

Bethany was preparing for Open House at her new school when Caleb called her as he usually did after getting off work.

"I have something to tell you. Do you want to know why it's so hard for me to leave Kacey?"

"I already know. You said she was there for you in one of the darkest times of your life."

"That's not the only reason," he said.

"Well, why? You already said that you weren't driving an hour for no damn body."

"We got engaged back in February on Valentine's day."

His confession produced an internal raging downpour. She yelled and screamed, called him every name in the book and then hung up on him. Caleb would call back. She would hang up on him over and over again.

He texted her.

> *Baby, engagement does not mean I got married. I'm not marrying her. Ever since you came back into my life, I knew she was not the one. Baby, please don't act like this.*

Bethany refused to communicate with him. She struggled with the news and tried to make a getaway from this cycle that continued to pierce her very soul.

After many failed attempts to reach her, Caleb texted Bethany that she was acting like a spoiled brat and that she needed to find someone else to help her move into the apartment.

When Bethany finally finished Open House and made it back to Lisel's, she broke down in tears as if someone she loved dearly had died.

"What's wrong Sis?" Lisel asked as she saw Bethany sitting in the car crying.

"He's freaking engaged."

"Who?"

"Caleb, sis."

"What! I knew something wasn't right about him."

"I hate him, sis. I hate him."

"You are going to be alright. C'mon out the car sis."

Bethany continuously cried and cried as she laid down on the bed. She told Lisel she needed time alone. This was definitely Bethany's style of grieving, but she was stuck with moving in a few days with no moving help from Huntsville to Newnan. Laying all embarrassment aside, Bethany called her mother to tell her the news. Her mother reassured her that helping her move was no problem, but now Bethany was faced with a decision; did she really want to move. For the next few days, she contemplated the very acts that seemed so divine and the current realities that made her feel less than a woman. She had had enough and didn't want to live anymore. She would wake up angry that she didn't die in her sleep.

As promised, Bethany received help moving from her family. It was a long day and a lot of driving, but they got her settled in. It had been four days since she had spoken to Caleb and even though she told herself that she would never speak to him again, she called him. Caleb knew her love for him ran deep. He knew how to finagle his way back, and he did. Caleb reassured Bethany that God made her for him and him for her, and ever since He brought her back in his life, he knew Kacey was not who he wanted to marry. Bethany believed what he said to be true and allowed the communication, the visits, and the sex to continue. Even though he swore he rarely had sex with Kacey, they never used protection. This was a habit that Bethany had begun to think about. Bethany didn't want to catch any sexually transmitted diseases, but she now wanted to use this to her advantage. A few occasions, Bethany had whispered to Caleb "stay inside me" as they made passionate love. Bethany secretly hoped that in her most fertile days she would become pregnant. Maybe this would make Caleb finally break things off with Kacey.

Meanwhile, Bethany had noticed a difference in her relationship with Caleb. Their routine of calling and texting had changed. She would text, only to wait hours before he responded. He denied that anything was wrong and claimed everything was fine. She knew something was not the same, but she believed him.

Lying across the bed one restless day with her phone in her hand, Bethany had started scrolling through her Facebook feeds to take her mind off Caleb and how weird he was acting. Immediately she stopped when she read "Don't be desperate for love. Love yourself more. Set standards and don't compromise. Real love takes time!" Real love is what Bethany thought she had found four years ago, but she had lowered her standards and compromised on things she thought she would never do.

After days of enduring Caleb's irregularities in his calls and texts, Bethany began to feel a little distant from him. She kept thinking about the quote she had read on Facebook. Wanting to talk through some things with him, she texted him.

Wyd.

About an hour had passed and still no response.

Caleb, are you okay?

Ten minutes later, he finally responded.

Just made it to Miami.

Bethany shouted, "What in the world!" Tears flowed down her face as a warm feeling covered her face. All while he had not committed to her, she had to accept that another woman was getting what she wanted from him. It should have been her who got the trips and vacations—not Kacey.

Bethany sent a reply.

Why didn't you tell me you were going out of town?

***

It didn't matter if I told you or not. That's why.

Caleb might as well have told Bethany that she did not matter. That's exactly how she felt.

It had been over four months since they'd last re-connected, and he still had not committed to a real relationship with her. Bethany didn't understand how he could say that he loved her, knowing that she was the woman God picked for him and yet still struggle to release his current relationship.

Bethany felt her heart break for what she vowed would be the last time. It had been broken, healed, then broken and healed again with this same man. At this point, she was not even bitter or upset. She did not want to argue with him about it. The questions that she had, she did not even have to have them answered. She just wanted to be free.

She wanted to be free from being the one who pleased him sexually. She wanted to be free from the guilt that he tried to place on her. She wanted to be free from his exploitation. She wanted to be free from his insecurities. She wanted to be free from being the one he relied on spiritually and emotionally. She used to wonder why God would allow them to reconnect and give her a job in Newnan, all while still not officially being together. But no more. She just wanted to be free. This was it!

Flipping through the pages of her journal, Bethany stopped and read what she wrote the first time her and Caleb ended their relationship.

A new chapter starts right now, not tomorrow morning. I will no longer feel like something is wrong with me just because of a man's insecurities. My new chapter is not about my desire for a husband and family. It is about walking in my freedom; loved and approved by God and myself.

Reading her own words produced the strength and confidence Bethany needed to do what had to be done one last time. So, she picked up the phone and dialed Caleb's number, knowing he would not answer because he was on vacation with his fiancée.

"You have reached the voicemail of Caleb Mitchell. Please leave a message after the beep."

"Caleb, I didn't want to text you this so, I called; I love you, but it's time I loved myself more. I can't do this anymore. I don't want to argue about it any longer. I am moving on."

Bethany ended the call and immediately blocked his calls and text messages. She knew talking to him would only lead to an argument that she was too tired to participate in.

Left alone to deal with the aftermath of her decision, she knew she had to do something different to prevent herself from finding an easy fix to take away the pain. This time she was going to sit in her pain and accept the truth instead of masking his lies with what she wanted to be true.

What if I am pregnant?

Bethany thought about her last sexual encounter with Caleb and knew it was a possibility. But now she had cut him off before confirmation of a positive or negative result.

Am I going to have to unblock his number and call him to tell him that I am pregnant? How will he respond? Will I be a single parent? Will I have to make him pay child support? How will we co-parent? All of these questions and more roamed through her mind.

Either way, she had made her decision, and she was sticking to it. No matter what, she did not think she would love him the same. He had simply forgotten to love her back.

To eliminate thoughts of Caleb and her recent actions, Bethany flipped on the television and watched the last five minutes of a daytime talk show. The words that were spoken resonated in her mind as she knew that in spite of her mistakes and failures, she still deserved to be pursued and loved.

As the show ended, Bethany burst into tears as she finally accepted that Caleb might as well have been dead to her. She moved into her sunroom where she often found peace and started to pray.

"God! I am broken. I need to be healed. I tried my own way, by attempting to control situations and people.

I have allowed others to manipulate and use my past against me to get what they wanted from me. I am tired, and I just want to be free from this."

Bethany continued her confessional prayer for almost half an hour. She had to confess every sin she could think of to Him, but she got up feeling free and confident that God would help her through her life's issues and provide real healing for her wounds.

Bethany ended her sobbing and prayer session by picking up her journal and writing a good-bye letter to her recycled love once and for all.

Dear Recycled Love,

Most people have decided to go green and recycle things like plastic, paper, and aluminum to help contribute to the Earth's overall health, and to keep the air, water, and land clean. I have tried to apply this same theory in love, but it tried to destroy my heart's overall health and polluted my mind, soul, and body. I have come to the realization that my love is not like plastic, paper, or aluminum. My love is more like new wine that should not be put in old bottles. Putting new wine in old bottles can cause the bottle to break and perish while the wine spills out.

I am cleaning up my spill today and to never make that mistake again. My love is too pure to have people treating it like water in a puddle on the streets. Today I choose to go back through the process of harvesting, crushing, pressing, fermentation, clarification, aging, and bottling again to receive my new love.

It was signed, *Bethany*.

***

STARING AT HER MENSTRUAL CYCLE CALENDAR again, Bethany counted her days in her head for the third time. Twenty-eight. Twenty-nine. Thirty. Thirty-one. Thirty-two. Thirty-three. "I can't be pregnant," she whispered a silent prayer, "Lord, please don't let me be." It had been two weeks since she had broken things off with Caleb and she had no intentions of getting back with him.

Bethany laid on her back in the middle of her bed with her eyes fixed on the ceiling. She glanced at her phone on the nightstand. It read 2:23 am. She exhaled and rolled onto her body pillow with her face buried inside her arms. Moments later, uncontrollable tears burst forth like water from a dam as she sat straight up with her legs in Indian style. She had thoughts of how disappointed her parents would be if she was pregnant. What would her Christian friends think of her? Did Caleb truly love her from the beginning? How would she support a child alone flooded her mind more than she realized. As she returned to her backside, she continued tossing and turning, as she also thought about Caleb's guilt-triggering email he sent after failed attempts of not reaching her on the phone. She blocked all calls and texts immediately after breaking things off with him on his voicemail. Reading his email stung Bethany deeply because she hoped against hope for a love she thought was destined to be all hers. With tears rolling down her face, she read Caleb's email for probably the 50th time.

I'm not surprised at all by you leaving me. All you know how to do is walk away. You give up so easily. Ain't nobody gonna be perfect. I deserve somebody who will be there for me, and that's what Kacey has done. I deserve her. She was there for me when I didn't have anything. You are so selfish to want me to up and leave her. You are just mad that you can't have me. You are getting just what you deserve. I'm not gonna allow you to walk in and out of my life anymore. Stay out of my life once and for all.

Did he really compare me to Kacey when all he has done is cheated on her with me? Bethany's chest tightened in anger. *Yes, Kacey had been there for him when he had pulmonary issues that required multiple biopsies, but she was his girlfriend. Isn't that what she was supposed to do? But she doesn't know about him cheating on her either. All those lies he told her to be with me,* Bethany continued to think to herself.

She tried to be there for Caleb too, but how could she when he had a girlfriend for the last two years. He'd never really allowed her to be there because he always had his guard up. She had even offered to nurse him back to health if his surgery was during the school's summer break. She never worked during the summer, after working summer school, following her first year of teaching. Bethany remembered getting burned out within the first couple of months after returning to the regular school year, and she promised herself to never work during the summer again.

Bethany wiped the tears from her eyes with the back of her hand, as she accepted the fact that not only was the relationship over, but the man she loved didn't love her back. There was nothing she could do about it. She contemplated emailing him to give him a piece of her mind, but she realized that closure isn't always necessary to end a relationship. Bethany picked up her phone to call her bestie Ne'cole. She knew it was too early in the morning, but she really needed her confidant.

After a few rings, Bethany heard a groggy, "Hello."

"Girl, I think I'm pregnant, my cycle is late."

"What!!! You lying."

'I'm serious Nikki."

"Wait! How many days?"

"Five."

"Girl, have you taken a test?"

"No, I bought one though. I'm waiting to take it first thing when I wake up. If I ever fall asleep."

"Beth, you gotta stop doing this to yourself. At least protect yourself."

"I know girl," Bethany sighed. "I hate to admit it, but I think part of me thought this would make him want me."

"How do you even know that he would be there for you and the child? Believe me, you don't want to go through what I am going through. Remember my story Bethany, I get no breaks."

ne'cole

NE'COLE MET HER SON'S father in college at the student center. The electronic bark of atomic dog traveled from the speakers mounted on the top corner of the student center's patio area. Three football players gathered around a study table to play Spades. Among the players were the infamous sophomore wide-receiver, Mars Hill.

His heart fluttered as he laid his eyes on the new girl on campus, Ne'cole Jones, walking with a group of her friends across the patio.

"Hey! Anybody wanna get in on dis Spades game?" one of the other guys yelled.

"The pretty girl with the hazel eyes wanna play," Mars shouted hoping to gain Ne'cole's attention.

Never breaking her stride, Ne'cole continued walking deliberately ignoring Mars' weak advances. Her auntie warned her how the athlete's prey on "fresh meat," so Ne'cole purposed not to be anybody's dinner.

Meanwhile, Mars bowed his head in defeat as the guys laughed at his failed attempt to get Ne'cole's attention.

Trying to soothe his bruised ego, *Maybe she didn't hear me,* Mars thought to himself.

"Where ya going?" shouted the boys at the card table.

"Gimme me a sec. I'll be right back."

Since Ne'cole was getting farther from him, he picked up a jog. When he finally caught up with her, he took a moment to wipe his sweaty hands on his shorts before speaking to her.

"Yo! Excuse me. Wanna play cards with us?"

"No thank you. I got class," Ne'cole responded with feigned apathy.

"May I carry your books for you then?"

"I can carry my own books, besides my class is right there."

"Can I at least get your name?" Mars asked desperately. "I'm Mars."

"See ya later Mars," Ne'cole said with a coy smile and walked away with her friends to the science building.

Mars faked a wide smile to avoid admitting that the conversation didn't go as planned with Ne'cole.

"Aight! Let's get dis game started," he said a little too loudly trying to regain his confidence.

"D'you get her number?"

"Not yet," Mars nodded as his devised his next plan in his head to gain Ne'cole's attention.

Running late on the first day of his psychology class, Mars' eyes lit up with excitement to see Ne'cole sitting on the front row of the stadium style classroom. He walked across the room to sit next to her. Ne'cole tsked tsked a silent disapproval to his tardiness. *Just like a typical jock,* she thought to herself.

"What's up Ne'cole," Mars whispered to her as he sat in the seat next to her.

"How do you know my name?"

Mars pointed to her name written so neatly on the top of her handout.

"Oh!" She softly giggled in her embarrassment.

Distracted with thoughts of being the potential boy-friend of the most beautiful girl on campus, Mars didn't pay much attention to the professor. Instead, he contemplated how to get Ne'cole's phone number when class ended.

"What class you got next?" Mars asked.

"I'm done for the day," Ne'cole responded coolly.

"Wanna grab lunch in the student center? I got you."

"I've got to study."

His usual tactics of courting weren't working with Ne'cole. A free meal worked on almost any girl.

Ne'cole, on the other hand, was hard to crack, but giving up pursuit was not an option. Her style and grace brought up a level of maturity that Mars had not displayed with his previous girlfriends. Recognizing he needed some advice, he sought wise counsel from his father as he strategized another plan.

He arrived the second day of psychology class on time and as predicted Ne'cole sat on the first row. He smiled inside as he took a seat beside her.

"Good afternoon Ne'cole."

"Hi, Mars," surprisingly finding herself flattered by his consistency.

Again, Mars found himself distracted throughout the lecture. He couldn't wait to give her the letter he wrote the night before.

When class ended, Mars discreetly laid an envelope inside of Ne'cole's books. He left class with renewed confidence that it wouldn't be too long before she would be his girl.

"What is that smell?" Ne'cole shouted laying across the bed in her dorm room.

She looked around perplexed by Uncle Tony's scent knowing he couldn't possibly be there.

She sniffed around like her mutt Rufus at home when he was on the hunt for a hidden bacon treat. Her nose lead her to the stack of books on the dresser. She opened the book to find the light blue envelope that was Uncle Tony's imposter. It simply read to Ne'cole from Mars. Laughing out loud, Ne'cole opened the envelope, and instantly her face warmed as she read the letter.

Dear Ne'cole,

I know this might seem strange, but I have been watching you and praying for an opportunity to get to know you. I wanted to let you know that I'm feeling your style. Here's my number. I hope that you would give me a call. If you don't, I'm not mad at you. We can still be cool.

It was signed, *Mars Hill.*

Goosebumps covered her arms as Ne'cole smiled like a smitten fourth grader who received that first "will you go out with me check yes or no" note. She laughed as she had heard similar words from Musiq Soulchild's song Just Friends. Now the blocks of the ice wall melted each time she read Mar's letter.

She changed her mind a million and one times before deciding what to do next. Three days was too long for another encounter, she thought to herself. So, Ne'cole picked up the phone and called him.

Four rings felt like an eternity before the deep voice answered, "Hello."

"May I please speak to Mars?"

"Speaking."

For some reason, his voice seemed almost musical and alluring like Gerald Levert singing Baby Hold On To Me, and it sounded even more mature than she remembered.

"This is Ne'cole."

"Of course. I know your voice."

"That's a sweet letter you wrote me."

"That's what's up. It's how I feel about ya; you are so beautiful to me."

"Thank you." Ne'cole just knew he could see her smiling through the phone.

"What's your classification?" Ne'cole curiously asked.

"I'm a sophomore. You're a freshman, right?"

"Yeah."

"Cool! Welcome to the Capstone."

The final chunk in her ice wall diminished, and all her guarded thoughts came spilling out.

"Thank ya! I like all my classes and professors. I've met some really cool people, and..."

Their conversation continued for hours. It was very obvious that both Mars and Ne'cole were enjoying the conversation. They talked about their majors, current classes, professors, and upcoming events on campus.

From that day on, it was hard for Ne'cole to hide her love for the sophomore football standout and soon it became hard to hide that baby bump he gave her too.

They both agreed life goals would not be derailed due to the pregnancy. Mars was attentive to Ne cole's needs, and they worked as a team to finish college with a child. After they graduated Mars and Ne'cole got married. Mars received a prestigious overseas opportunity in Asia. Ne'cole and Malik rarely saw Mars due to his demanding position at the American company with a base in Singapore. They divorced years later due to the strain, and ultimately it left Ne'cole to raise their son on her own.

***

"I know it was stupid Nikki, thinking back on all this, but now I just have to wait and see at this point."

"Either way it will be okay. I'm your girl, and I got your back."

"Thanks, girl."

Bethany felt a little better after talking and listening to her girl, Ne'cole, but she continued to toss and turn for over an hour. She considered things that could help her sleep, like Advil PM, but as she pulled the bottle out of the medicine cabinet, the bottle was empty. Walking in the kitchen, she spotted her favorite bottle of muscadine wine. After wine tasting with Ne'cole at a prominent Atlanta GA vineyard, she fell in love with this light yet sweet wine that had been missing all of her adult life. *That's what I need to relax me,* she thought to herself. But suddenly the thought of being pregnant returned and she definitely didn't want to harm the baby. *Baby! Oh my God*, she thought as she stood frozen in front of the wine rack. *How could I be so stupid? Lord, please don't let me be pregnant. I promise if I am not pregnant I will not have sex again until I am married.*

Coming to no reasonable answer, she returned to the bed and just laid there until she finally fell asleep. Hours later she was awakened by her Russian flag as her African friend Joseph called it. She did not mind the cramps and back pain this month. She was just happy that she got her period and that she wasn't pregnant. She vowed to herself and God that this was the final chapter with her love affair with Caleb. She had dodged a major bullet, and she was not about to play Russian roulette with Caleb again.

chapter six

READY TO BEGIN A new life, Bethany began to search for a new hairstyle and a stylist who could bring it to life. She remembered an episode of the housewives where the ladies were styled by Jazzy, the most popular stylist in Atlanta. She was known for her creative cuts; she had over a million followers on Instagram and had women looking like superstars. Just her luck, Jazzy was taking new clients, and Bethany booked her appointment online.

Sitting in the car, Bethany touched her long healthy black hair once more before walking into the salon. She wanted a completely new look. Jazzy greeted her as she walked in.

"Hello, beautiful. I'm Jazzy."

"Hi. I'm Bethany."

"Oh yes. You are my 2 o'clock. Right this way."

Jazzy escorted Bethany to her chair.

"What are we getting today?"

"Cut it off!" Bethany said as she flopped into Jazzy's salon chair. She pulled a picture up on her phone and showed Jazzy a picture of Megan Good. "I want it short like this."

"Are you sure Bethany? Your hair is so long and healthy." Jazzy doubled checked as she always did with her new clients.

Bethany hadn't let herself think about it deeply, but she needed to be someone other than the woman who wasn't good enough for Caleb. Since she couldn't change her weight immediately, the go-to was her hair. It's something about a woman changing her hair that made her feel brand new.

"Okay, miss lady. At your command."

Jazzy was as good as the reviews said she was. Bethany absolutely loved her cut and felt young and free.

"Do you like it girl?"

"Absolutely. You just became my new stylist."

"Great! I love when my clients walk out totally satisfied."

Bethany couldn't wait to facetime her bestie to flaunt her new look and to secretly get her approval.

"Look at you hot mama," came Ne'cole's voice from the FaceTime screen.

"How you like it?"

"You look amazing girl. What made you cut your hair, Beth?"

"I'm in a new city, and I got a new attitude. I can't keep letting Caleb drag me through these cycles that leave my heart broken into pieces. He got his girl. Now that I know I'm not pregnant by him, it's time for me to find me some business." Bethany gained a spark of confidence with her "Stella Got Her Groove Back" speech.

"I love it. You are so smart and beautiful, and you deserve so much more."

Bethany appreciated having Ne'cole as her bestie and silent confidant during her recycled love experience with Caleb. She never told her what to do, but silently walked through it all with her. On the other hand, Ne'cole was also Bethany's cheerleader, and she always could count on her to boost her confidence at least when they weren't both making a mess of their lives at the same time.

"Thank you, girl." Bethany excitedly responded.

Bethany always heard that the best way to get over one man was to find another man. She tried not to let the pain of losing Caleb get to her, for she was not completely over him. She started and erased many texts messages to him during her lonely nights in the apartment that was supposed to be shared by both of them. She found herself becoming angrier with God for reconnecting them only for Caleb to deceive her. For weeks, Bethany came home from worked and cried herself to sleep thinking about the fool she had been for love. She might have changed her hair, but her heart remained in love with him.

Since she never died in her sleep, she knew she still had a life to live. In her continual efforts to get over Caleb, Bethany joined the gym. Being a little insecure of her curves, she knew she would have to drop about thirty pounds to compete with the smaller frame women that looked like video girls.

Although she was a beautiful woman, Bethany struggled with her self-confidence. She secretly counted herself out anytime her and Ne'cole would hang out. Ne'cole had the small waist and big butt that she thought every man preferred. Caleb would serenade her all the time with how perfect her body was, but she never believed it. Her grandmother used to tell her all the time that she was too big, and when she lost weight she didn't look right. No matter what size she was, Bethany had grown to not like her appearance, but joining a gym was also a place where she would see a lot of men to hopefully find her some new business.

Bethany didn't have any real luck meeting men out and about in her new community, but every time she went to the local gym her eyes were destined to find a prize. After a month or so, she still had no luck, but things were getting tighter, toner, and higher by the day. Her butt and her confidence were rising like one of her grandmother's buttermilk biscuits. She wanted to post her progress on her Instagram so that Caleb could see what he was missing, but she had blocked him the day she read his nasty email. It was probably for the best though. She needed that space to heal from him.

"How's the man search going Beth?" Ne'cole casually queried during their morning car phone conversations before work.

"Not that good. Where do you meet guys nowadays?"

"You know online dating is hot these days, but that is not my cup of tea."

"Yeah, I have heard of some of the sites and seen the commercials. Did you know Caleb met Kacey online?"

"I didn't." Ne'cole almost regretted bringing it up.

"Yep! Maybe I should give it a try too." Bethany said with excitement in her voice. "I could post my pictures from our spring break trip and take some pictures with my new haircut. Surely, I can meet some guys this way."

Ne'cole was relieved to hear Bethany's spunk.

"Go head girl! Just be careful." There was a silence that lasted for about five seconds. "Bethany?" No answer. "Hello?"

"Oh, I'm sorry girl. I was trying to find that picture of me in my black wrap dress and leopard print heels. I hear you Ne'cole. I will be careful."

Bethany couldn't wait to get home that evening to set-up her online dating profile. She looked through her pictures off and on at work trying to decide which ones to post. She chose one formal wear, one casual wear, one with her glasses, and of course, one in her favorite black wrap dress; the one she wore when she first saw Caleb at a Sunday service at City View back in Huntsville.

Hmmm, what do I want my username to be? Bethany thought as she stared at the setup page. It seemed like every name she tried was already taken. Best Kept Secret. Beautiful Lady. Single Young and Beautiful. She spent about ten minutes just thinking of a username until she tried Positively New 16. Nobody had taken that name. Bethany hoped it reflected her new attitude toward embracing a new city, a new look, and possibly a new man in twenty-sixteen.

"Really!" shouted Bethany at the screen as she clicked the next page. Even though Bethany enjoyed writing and had written her own book she found it very difficult to write about herself in the "tell us about you" section of the profile. She flopped back on her pillow, closed her eyes, and blew out a long-frustrated sigh before she proceeded to write about herself.

> *Starting over in a new city can be challenging, but I am embracing the new with a positive attitude. I have been in Coweta County for about five months. I am in my mid-thirties. I am single with no kids. I work in education, and I have a newfound love of writing. I would consider myself an introvert with extrovert tendencies. I enjoy the simple things in life that bring the greatest joys such as walks in the park, movies, bowling, spending time with family and friends, etc. I would love to meet a man who is mature and stable,*

enjoys comedy, and who believes in the power of love. Cheers to the possibility of great conversations and the beginning of a great friendship that will last forever.

With the online dating profile complete, Bethany was instructed as she viewed men pictures to swipe left for not interested and right for "are you my new man?"

Starting her new journey seemed harder than she imagined. After a few days of swiping through on-line profiles, she barely came across anyone she was interested in. She was overwhelmed with the millions of flirty winks received on a daily basis and the one-word direct messages of "hey." Which made her think *Are we in grade school?* She was confused. There were a few guys that caught her eye and as nervous as she was about making the first move, she initiated the conversation.

How are you? My name is Bethany. I found your pictures and profile attractive. Would you like to chat?

Sometimes hours would pass and even a few days be-fore she would hear a reply as simple as "sure." "That's it! After all I wrote, that's all he had to say." This was bad but not as bad as when the conversation seemed to be going great, and all of the sudden communica-tion ceased altogether. He went ghost. Occasionally, she encountered the surprising yet honest men who were only looking for a friend with benefits.

Frustration was building in her online search, and she decided to give it a break for a while. She finally decided to take her co-worker, Jocelyn, up on her invitation to meet for drinks at a local Mexican spot.

"So, how are you liking Rising Star so far?"

"I'm still getting adjusted, but I like it."

"You came from Alabama right?"

"Yes, Huntsville."

"What brought you here?"

"Just needed a change and I'm a little closer to family."

"Cool. How is Newnan treating you?"

"Well, I really haven't done much?"

"Girl, you gotta get out. It's a lot to do here."

"Yeah, I know."

"Are you dating?"

Bethany released a long sigh and responded, "I wish."

"Me either girl. I'm on a couple of dating sites, and it's crazy."

"Omgeee. I just signed up, and there are some weirdos."

"Yeah, I know what you are talking about."

"One guy sent me a picture of his penis and said hello sexy."

Jocelyn laughed as she knew Bethany was not lying.

"That has happened to me too, and it seems like the fine guys don't respond."

"Yes, girl. Maybe too many women hit them up, and they have options."

"How long have you been single Jocelyn?"

"Girl, I am thirty-eight. Never been married and no kids. I dated this guy for about two years, and we broke up because he wasn't trying to get married. Ever since then it has been hard to find a decent man. What about you?"

"I have had my shares ups and downs. A guy I dated off and on turned out to not be who I thought he was."

"Men can be such liars."

Bethany nodded in agreeance. "Are there any places around here to meet guys?"

"There is. You just have to be careful here. A lot of the men are bisexual."

"Yeah, so I have been told."

"My church is having a single's Meetup next Friday if you want to go."

"Nah, I pass. Most of the time single's ministries is just another women's ministry from my perspective."

"Girl, you ain't never lied. The last meetup with had, three guys showed up, and there were about a hundred women."

"It was the same in Huntsville too. Why do you think so many women are single these days?"

"Your guess is just as good as mine. As for me, I don't have time to raise a man. I need him to come ready. Most of these guys our age are just now getting themselves together. Shoot, I ran across this one guy online. Fine as hell, but he had four children and in school. Hell Naw. I'm not waiting on him. I want to travel and have fun."

"I feel you girl."

"Listen, I told God that actually, I was okay being single as long as I could get some every now and then."

"No, you didn't."

"Yes, I did. You have to keep it real with God. He knows my heart."

"Jocelyn, you are crazy, girl."

"I'm just saying."

The waitress brought over their checks as they had finished their third round of margaritas.

"Listen, Bethany welcome to Newnan. Rising Star can get crazy sometime so let me know if you need anything. We need to do this again."

Bethany and Jocelyn parted ways after a much-needed girls' time. Jocelyn was the first friend she met at work and in the city; it was good to know she was not alone. However, alone is just what she felt when she made it back to her empty apartment.

Surely there was someone who could be a company keeper. As she scrolled through her contacts list, her fingers landed on the first man she thought would be her husband, Nick. She had heard through the grapevine that he was divorced, and his ex-wife and his kids moved to Nevada. Even though she would never trust him again or wanted a relationship with him, she thought he would be a great pacifier, someone to meet her urging needs and smooth over the sharp edges of her growing loneliness. She hadn't talked to him in over a year, but she was desperate and hated to admit it.

Before she knew it, she had dialed his number. *What do I say? "Hi, it's me," or, "what's up?"* The phone rang three, four, five times. *Great, here comes voicemail.*

Bethany, desperate, lonely, and greatly in need of some physical attention almost laughed picturing herself with a sign, "Will Cook for Hugs."

A deep voice broke her thoughts.

"Wassup, stranger!"

"Hey, Nick. How are you?" Bethany felt a little guilty because she knew there was so much behind her casual hey.

"I'm good. Where have you been?"

"I've been around. Just working. Recently moved to Newnan."

"Oh yeah!"

"Yeah."

"You are a little closer to me now, huh?"

"I guess I am."

"I'm surprised to hear from you. I have tried to reach out to you a few times."

"Yeah, I apologize. I've been going through some things, but I miss talking to you."

"Is that so?" He was making her work harder than she wanted to, but he was so sexy.

"Yes. I really enjoyed the time we spent together. We had something special."

"We really did."

Bethany and Nick were the epitome of a successful long-distance relationship. They saw each other every other weekend. Most of the time, Nick came to see her in Huntsville. A fun, passionate, friendship best described what they had; from weekends of playing racquetball, visiting art and historical museums, spring break cruises, a peaceful night sipping wine, reviewing new restaurants or just sleeping in, these two had quite a fun-filled relationship. Multiple times a day, they engaged in conversations that aided in the trust and communication needed for any romantic relationship. It was like fireworks each time they kissed, and passion filled their most intimate moments together. That's why it hurt like hell the day she found out he was still married. *How could he do this to me?* she thought; shame and hurt caused her to go cold turkey on a love she thought was so real.

Now after four and a half years, Bethany and Nick talked for over an hour that night reminiscing about the details of their former relationship.

"So, when are you gonna invite me to Newnan?"

"One day."

She didn't want to start anything with Nick again. She just needed someone to take her mind off of Caleb.

"Well, I look forward to that day."

Meanwhile, Bethany continued her swiping. She couldn't stand getting the messages from guys that read, "Hey Sexy." She immediately deleted those guys from her list. She couldn't believe the guys who messaged her with gold grills on their teeth and braids plaited to the back of their head. She deleted them too. She didn't worry too much because she texted Nick whenever she needed the attention of a man.

"So, when I'm gonna see you Baby?" Nick asked after two weeks of talking with Bethany. He was never the one to hesitate to ask for what he wanted; she remembered she found that very sexy at one time.

Bethany knew she didn't want the same thing as Nick, but she decided to play the role and agreed to go see him. She dare not invite him to her place. She desired a fresh beginning with a renewed state of mind, in her new city. She wanted to control when and how she actually required her pacifier of a man.

"I'll be down your way on Saturday. I'll drop by and spend some time with you."

Bethany knew deep down this would be temptation land. She has always been attracted to Nick's smooth and classic pretty boy yet athletic look. How would she resist him when lately she had been hot and horny? She had been desperately missing the pleasures of the body she got from Caleb.

"I can't wait to see you Babe."

"Good. I'll talk to you a little later okay."

Moments after she hung up with Nick, Bethany heard the notification sound coming from her phone. She tsked loudly and hissed her annoyance as she crossed the room to get her phone.

"Didn't I tell him I would talk to him lately," she hissed. "He always had to push too hard. That's why we…"

Bethany paused when she saw it was a notification from her online dating app. She opened the app and read her new message from loverboy_84.

Hello, Ms. Positively New 16. My name is Roman, and I must say that your profile really caught my eye. I would love to chat with you if you are interested.

Hmmm? Bethany smiled. "What does this young buck want with me?" Bethany hurriedly pulled up his profile; tapped and scrolled through his information to see if he was worth her response. She did appreciate the fact that he used correct grammar, and he messaged her more than "Hey." She wasn't sure whether to put that in the positive or negative. He was literally a shorty. Only two inches taller than Bethany. "Shoot, I can't wear heels with him." Bethany laughed as she began to read his profile. He had three major pluses: college grad, never married, and no kids—jackpot!

What the heck? She tapped the message space and the dialogue between them bubbled over.

Hey Roman. My name is Bethany. It is a pleasure hearing from you. How are you today?

***

Much better since you have responded. His response was immediate.

"That's cute," chuckled Bethany as she tapped out her response.

So, what on my profile caught your attention?

***

First and foremost, you are absolutely beautiful.

***

Thank you. Your pictures were eye-catching as well.

***

Thanks. So, are you single?

***

Of course. I wouldn't be on the site if I wasn't.

***

Believe me, I have ran into a lot of married women on here.

***

No way.

***

Yep. I'm not trying to get down like that.

***

I know that's right. So, I'm assuming you are single too.

***

I am very single.

***

Are you hetero, homo, or bisexual?

***

lol. I'm not interested in any men dear. I love women only.

***

Okay. I just have to ask these days. What's your dating style?

***

What do you mean?

***

Do you date multiple people?

***

I like to get to know one woman at a time.

His response took Bethany by surprise. Not many people nowadays had this style of dating. She wasn't quite sure this was her new style after all she had been through, but this was definitely her traditional way of dating.

Cool. Any kids?

***

Nope. You?

***

No kids.

***

I guess we have something in common.

***

lol. I guess so.

Bethany thought she was dreaming. She hasn't dated a man without kids since her first college boyfriend. She thought maybe her past experiences led her to what she ultimately desired in a man from the very beginning.

For the next two hours, Bethany gained his perspectives on education, family, and politics. Within thirty minutes, he managed to get her number; she hadn't given out her number since she began the world of online dating. It was something about Roman that slowly caused her heart to hope again in the possibility of love. After three days of hour-long conversations, he invited her to coffee and Bethany agreed to step out a little on the limb.

Arriving early, as usual, Bethany found a quiet corner with a window for them to sit. She was always the first to arrive at work and even at social gatherings. It was, in her opinion, a quality more people should possess, then CP Time wouldn't be such a joke. But today, it was working against her. It gave her more time to drive herself crazy. *What if I'm not attracted to him? What if he catfish me? What if he is missing a tooth? What if he's already here watching me?* All these thoughts bumrushed her mind, and she sipped more of her tea to calm herself. To busy her thoughts, she pulled out her phone to text Ne'cole.

Girl, I'm so nervous.

***

You so silly Beth. There is no need to be. Just try to enjoy the moment. You got this girl.

***

So, you say, pray for me girl.

***

ttyl

As Bethany tucked her phone away, she felt someone's eyes on her. At the very same moment, Bethany's eyes raised as she could smell his alluring scent ten feet away. There he stood five foot nine of pure sexiness. Jet black wavy hair with a meticulously edged fade. Arm muscles tugged against the sleeves of his fitted T-shirt like a human mountain range from arm to chest to his other arm. Hmmm, Bethany almost licked her lips LL Cool J style as her eyes ran across his smooth lips framed by a neatly lined goatee. His deep dark eyes perused the room until it locked with hers. Bethany gave him a wave with a flirty smile that led him her way. She stood to hug him and soon melted into the mountains.

"You're even more beautiful in person," he charmingly said to Bethany.

"You're quite handsome in person yourself." Bethany always seemed to know what to say in the moment. She was quite a flirt.

After the witty flirtation broke the ice, Roman led Bethany to the cashier where she ordered her Strawberry Lemonade Refresher. All of the nervousness was gone, and she often found herself feeling like she already had established puppy love with him. Their conversation was natural, and it was if they picked up where they left off on the phone.

Her butterflies were interrupted by a buzzing sound from her purse. She reached in to silence the vibrating annoyance that was interrupting her Brown Sugar moment. When she saw Nick's name, she almost gasped and silenced it quickly.

"Is everything alright?" Roman asked, and she prayed he hadn't seen anything panicky on her face.

"Yes, of course." She regrouped, sipping her lemonade and drinking him in with her eyes. She looked and smiled blushingly at the cutie who sat across from her.

Roman was attractive, no question about that, but he was a few years younger than Bethany and a little shorter than what she preferred. He had all of the other criteria she wanted and didn't want to lose a potentially good man over height and age.

He continued to shower Bethany with compliments about her beauty. Her weight was not even an issue for him even though she was a little self-conscious about it. When she mentioned losing weight, Roman agreed to workout and even eat healthy with her. He told Bethany that he looks at the heart of a person because the weight can be lost. He was definitely melting her heart.

"Can I see you again?" Roman asked Bethany at the end of their meet and greet.

"I would like that," Bethany smiled as she replied.

Nick must have called and texted Bethany about twenty times that day, but she ignored them all. She did not need a pacifier right now. Later that night, Roman called to ask if he could come over to see her again. After dealing with months of loneliness and craving for a new love, Bethany was ecstatic. So, she texted him her address, and he arrived about an hour later.

"Why you have a guard up?" Roman asked Bethany sitting across from him on the sofa.

"I don't have a guard," Bethany blushed.

"I like you Bethany and want to know everything about you," Roman assured her as he inched in closer.

"I like you too."

"So, relax," Roman said as he leaned in to kiss Bethany.

Bethany let her guard fall and passionately returned the kiss. He took her hands and wrapped them around his neck, and his hands moved slowly over her back to her hips.

"Wait," she said as she pulled away from him.

"We are moving too fast."

Roman's response was like he didn't even hear her, and his tongue probed deeper. If a mouth had a G spot he found it, and she hypnotically followed; he stood up, reached for her hand, and led her to her bedroom.

"Oh my God! I can't believe I had sex with a man I have only known for a few days." For the next hour, on her bed, Bethany tossed back and forth in her mind between condemnation and satisfaction. Ultimately Roman's performance won out, and Bethany enjoyed the moment of feeling wanted.

chapter seven

FOR THE NEXT FEW weeks, Bethany saw Roman every other night while still ignoring the calls and texts from Nick.

Are you okay Babe? So, you aren't gonna answer my call. Wyd? Call me. He flooded her phone almost daily.

Bethany wanted to reply, but she didn't want to tell Nick what she had really been up to, and she didn't want to mess things up with Roman. She was really falling quickly for Roman who was so satisfying with his good looks, intellectual conversations, and of course, his magic stick. They didn't go out on many dates because of Roman's work schedule; at least that's what he told her. Managing a prestigious Business Club in the city took a lot of his time and allowed him to put his Master's degree to good use. Bethany tried to understand his work, but she couldn't wrap her mind around why the communication lessened by the day. It would be hours before he responded to her calls or texts.

Can I come to see you at your place when you get off?

107

Bethany texted out of curiosity. During the month, of seeing each other, she had never seen his place.

When I move to my new place in two months.

He texted about an hour later.

So, she asked the hard question, *Are you really single?*

Bethany began to feel like something wasn't quite right about the situation.

Three hours later he texted, *Yes.*

Not able to shake the feeling, Bethany texted him back.

Roman, stop playing with me.

Immediately he called. "Baby, I told you my place isn't ready to move in; it will be in two months. I am staying with two of my boys right now. I'm not playing with you."

Bethany felt a little guilty for assuming the worst and couldn't find the words to say that she was sorry.

"Baby, I told you that I want to be with you and only you. Don't categorize me with other men. That's how you push me away." The edge in his voice was only faintly masked.

"I'm sorry, but you were showing some tell-tale signs," Bethany said in a softer voice that she hoped didn't sound too desperate.

"I forgive you, Baby. I got to get back to work, but I'll see you tonight."

Roman came to see Bethany as he said that night. He wasted no time devouring her clothes off of her and laying the law down in the bedroom.

"Turn over," he authoritatively said.

Bethany turned over on her hands and knees, and his finger found its way into her mouth as he exerted an exotic force from behind. Satisfied was an understatement when it came to the pleasure Roman provided, but it still did not diminish the longing she had for quality time and her intuition about his lack of communication. Content, she suppressed her intuition that night and for the next three days until she just couldn't. On day four, she called repeatedly determined he wouldn't get the easy way out. Finally, at eight in the evening he picked up, and Bethany went straight for the jugular.

"So, I guess instead you are gonna push me away. I let down my guard for you because I liked you. I understand you work a lot, but you didn't have to do me like this for a piece of ass. I believed you and gave you the benefit of the doubt. It's okay if you became interested in somebody else, but you could have simply told me. Anyways, take care."

"Wait a minute Baby. I'm just getting off. I care about you."

"I care about you too. It just seems like you are extremely occupied."

"Stop assuming."

"I'm not assuming."

"All I do is work and go home."

"What about communication with me? I have been working on being patient. Most days I wouldn't hear from you if I didn't text or call. That makes me feel some type of way. I was taught that a man is gonna call if he wants you. Despite being told that, I believed you when you said you were interested, but I need to be shown that."

"Baby, I have been single for a long time. I'm gonna work on it. I'm sorry."

Bethany believed him and tried to look beyond her selfishness for the sake of companionship. But she was still feeling lonely. She honestly believed that his "working on it" would mean an increase of calls, dates, and visits. Ironically, they decreased. It was becoming too much; she needed a sounding board. Although Bethany had hardly mentioned Roman to Ne'cole, she needed relief from the growing loneliness. She dared not tell her that she quickly gave herself to someone she barely knew, so she shared the credentials she admired about him such as his Master's degree, no kids, his good looks, diverse conversation, physically fit, and of course, the one magical date he took her on. Bethany was thrilled to share the details of the private couples' massage Roman took her to with Ne'cole. It had been a while since she had even been on a date and this was definitely a step above dinner and a movie. But all that was a month ago now.

She pressed on, "Nikki, he was such a gentleman. He escorted me to this resort on the outskirts of the city for some rest and relaxation. We had our own private room for full body massages."

"Now that's sweet and thoughtful," Ne'cole said happily.

"And the complimentary refreshments... let me just say this Girl, I felt like royalty. The only complaint I have with him is communication and his work schedule. He doesn't like to talk on the phone, and he works around the clock."

"Sounds like he needs someone as busy as he is."

"I guess so, but it takes time and energy to build a relationship."

"That's so true."

"Well, one day at a time," Bethany sighed unconvinced.

"One day at a time," Ne'cole repeated. "See you in a week at the baby shower."

"See you then."

Bethany was not a woman who kept her feelings inside, but after not seeing Roman in over a week and a few random "I miss you" text she decided to try a different approach.

Hey Cutie, she texted him. *Come stay with me tonight.*

I will very soon, he replied almost two hours later.

I guess that's a no, she frustratingly texted back.

There was no response from Roman. Four hours later, Bethany called him only to get his voicemail as usual. Knowing she would get a quicker response with text she sent her message that way.

> *I can't compete with your job anymore or whatever else you have going on. I don't want to be friends with benefits. I tried to believe that you cared about me and that you were interested. I tried to believe that you were gonna work on communication. When you improved, I tried to affirm you, but it only lasted a day. I'm not desperate, and I gave you your space, but it seems like you need a lot of space from me. I don't know how to handle that. Only you and God knows when I would ever talk to you so, I texted this message.*

The next morning, Roman called to tell her the things she said in her message were not true. He had nobody else and was only dating her. He continued to mention that he has to work on it and that he really missed her. "Don't leave me Baby," he begged of her.

"You have to learn how to communicate Roman."

"I know Baby. I got to work on that. I'm not used to having someone in my life so, I don't think about stopping to check on anyone. When I get to work, I'm in work mode. I really care about you, and I'm not playing games with you."

Bethany pondered the internal battles she constantly fought within herself after her call from Roman. She didn't want to be known as the bitter black woman or the nagging woman, but she also didn't want to be anyone's fool. She had no evidence that he wasn't telling her the truth. *He does have a demanding job,* she kept telling herself.

Meanwhile, the day had arrived for the baby shower. She would see Ne'cole and her other college friends. She drove about an hour to celebrate with their friend, Dee Dee. The shower was awesome, color coordinated and overflowing with gifts and friends, but Bethany struggled internally. All her friends were with their husbands or beaus while her man hadn't even checked on her that day. She was trying to refrain from calling or texting him so, she checked her phone to see if he had initiated communication, but he hadn't.

On the road back to Newnan, she gave him a call, but there still was no answer. An hour later he texted, *How are you?* Bethany was heartbroken and didn't respond. Whatever they had was over for her.

Like a true friend, Ne'cole called soon after to make sure Bethany made it home okay.

"Everything ok girl?"

"Yeah," Bethany replied, "just made it in about ten minutes ago."

"Are you sure? You seemed a little off at the shower."

"I know—I just have some things to work out."

"You mean Roman?"

"Yeah."

"Well, don't trip too hard. Maybe some girlfriend time will help."

"Maybe."

"Look, I'm going to send you an invite to a bowling mixer next week in Columbus—say you'll come."

"I don't know Nikki."

"Please…it was so good to see you, but the time was too short. Heck, there may be someone there to take your mind off Roman for a minute."

"I don't know…I'll see."

"Okay, that's a yes, bye girl, love ya."

And in true Nikki fashion, the text was there inside her messages the next minute. The flyer: drinks, snacks, music, and bowling. *Maybe,* thought Bethany, *I need something else to do with myself.* Then a second text with a group photo. Several women and two guys, everyone smiling. It did look fun. One guy was pretty sexy looking too. *No, enough,* thought Bethany. *I've had enough. I have to stop running and sit in this misery.*

The ringing of her phone woke her up early the next morning. It was Roman, but she didn't answer. He immediately called again, and she still didn't answer. Rather she simply texted him that it was over.

As she rolled on her back into the bed, her eyes penetrated the ceiling as she thought about how she was starting the healing process again. Truth be told, she would have been starting it again even if there was no Roman because she used Nick to fill her emptiness before him.

Doing what she knew best to deal with life's disappointments, she reached for her journal and pen out of her nightstand and began to write:

Dear Open Wound,

I apologize for interrupting your healing process. The scab that would cover you was not a good look or feeling for me, so I picked it off every time. I didn't value that the scab formation was actually a sign that healing was taking place. Instead I delayed the process, and unfortunately, we are starting over. Forgive me for trying to rush the process and exposing you to harmful people. While I can't do anything to undo my previous actions, I can start today and allow the entire process to be completed. Let the stages of healing begin.

It was signed, *Bethany.*

chapter eight

BETHANY PULLED UP TO Barnes and Nobles and parked the car. Once one of her favorite spots to write, but now they were selling her very own book. Her eyes immediately found the flyer on the door advertising her latest book Love's Lottery. Tears rolled down her face as she remembered her humble beginnings as a writer and how she had succeeded in accomplishing that longtime dream of hers. Just last month, she was featured as Newnan's new rising best-selling author in the Metro-Atlanta Herald. Life was good, and she had one more novel to write to fulfill her book deal with her publishing company. She grabbed her purse and keys and opened the door, but her legs must have been paralyzed because she couldn't move, but her thoughts could. They rapidly crashed like tidal waves against her mind as she wondered why Caleb wanted to meet her here to talk.

Just a few days ago, Bethany opened her journal and began to write...

How do you know you have truly heard from God?

It had been a couple of months since Bethany broke things off with Caleb and just a few weeks of ending her erotic fling with Roman.

> *I really believed that it was the will of God for Caleb and me to be together after our last reconnection. I was fully persuaded by our conversation, and when things started to line up for me to be in the same city as him, I had no doubt that this was a God-thing,* she continued to write in her journal as she laid at the foot her empty California king bed.

Her thoughts were suddenly interrupted with vibrations from her phone.

"Hey, Necy!"

"Hey, Bestie. What are you up to?"

"Just doing a little journaling. What's going on?"

"I was just checking on you girl. You've been M.I.A."

Bethany chuckled at the truth. When she decided to truly heal from Caleb and Roman, she knew she would have to sit in her pain and just deal with it. Her morning routine calls to Ne'cole decreased and was replaced with meditations and devotions that focused on healing the heart.

"I'm still alive, girlie."

"But, how are you really doing?"

Tired of wearing the mask with the one friend she knew loved her dearly, Bethany busted into tears and decided to allow Ne'cole to feel her pain. Life goes on is what she had always told herself. So, moving on is all she had focused on since her breakup with Caleb, but she had forgotten one vital part of the healing process. Grieving.

With a squeaky voice and tears streaming down her face, she began to speak the words to describe her pain.

"I'm mad as hell. I know God doesn't make mistakes so, it had to be me, Nikki. I saw signs after I got the job in Newnan, but I was so sure that this was God's will that I ignored the signs."

"Are you mad at God?"

"I…I don't know. Yes. No. Not really. I guess I'm upset with myself. How could I be so stupid?"

"You're not stupid, Bethany."

"Why do I feel stupid then?"

"Honey." Ne'cole heavy sigh was heard through the phone as she slowly answered Bethany's question. "Love makes us feel this way sometimes, and you really loved Caleb."

"But why me?" Bethany flopped back on her bed like a spoiled two-year-old who couldn't get her way. "Why do I have to be the one who gets hurt while they go on with their merry lives?"

"Beth, who's to say that they are really happy."

"At least they got somebody."

"Listen girlie. I don't mean to sound preachy, because you know I struggle to walk the straight and narrow," Ne'cole jokingly said. "But Beth, our choices can also make us feel this way when they don't work out our preferred way; but honey, we all have played "a fool" for love a time or two."

Bethany found the strength to laugh at the comedian Ne'cole was trying to be. "That's so true."

"You remember what I went through with Chad, right?"

"Yeah, I remember."

"And Tony."

"Girl, you were crazy in love with him, and I thought you had nearly lost your mind."

They both laughed over those reminiscing thoughts of being stupid and in love.

"I survived the pain those jokers caused and healed, and Beth, you were right there with me."

"Of course, you are my girl. That's what friends are for."

"And Ms. Monroe, I'm gonna be right here with you."

"Thanks, friend."

Bethany was used to being there for Ne'cole and everyone else including herself. It was a big deal for her to share her deepest thoughts and disappointments with her best friend of sixteen years. But now her healing was more important than her pride, and she truly accepted she didn't have to do life alone.

Feeling encouraged by her talk with Ne'cole, Bethany decided to attend a worship service at the church around the corner from her new place. She had visited before and enjoyed the multi-cultural, modern day feel of the place. The late service started at noon, and she had just enough time to make it.

After a quick shower, Bethany put on her jeans with a white tee and her navy-blue blazer with her favorite brown boots and headed out the door. She was a natural beauty and didn't wear much foundation, but she did add some eyeliner and lip gloss in the car. Before entering the building, she quietly prayed in the car. "Lord, speak to me. I put my heart in Your hands." Grabbing her brown leather Bible and her purse, she got out the car and headed inside.

"Hello. Welcome to Freedom Chapel," one of the greeters opened the door and ushered her in.

"Thank you so much." Bethany smiled and followed the usher to her seat.

"Is this seat okay?" The usher asked.

Bethany didn't like sitting too close to the front or in the very back so, this middle section was perfect for her.

"Yes, thank you," Bethany replied.

While waiting for service to begin, Bethany grabbed an offering envelope and started to complete it.

"Here is a seat right here sir," she heard coming from behind her.

Her face lit up as she looked up to see a 6 foot 2, ripped jeans, white tee wearing, caramel colored complexion man with a Bible in his hands coming to sit next to her. *You gotta be kidding God.* She laughed at the thought that God had answered her prayers already by sending this gorgeous Jonathan biblical-like character to sit beside her.

"Good morning!" He spoke to her as he sat down.

"Good morning." Bethany purposed to stay focused on why she came to church this morning, so she didn't engage in much conversation. At least not with him, but in her head, she questioned was this the man God had prepared for her. Nah, stay focus girl. She told herself as the service began.

The worship leader asked everyone to stand, and the band started playing one of her favorite songs, "At the cross." Truth be told, she had a few things that she needed to lay at the cross. She lifted her hands to God and decided that without understanding every detail of what happened; she released the hurt from Nick, Caleb, and Roman from her hands.

After the church announcements, the band sung one more song before the middle-aged bi-racial preacher with khakis and a blue and brown pullover sweater took the stage.

"Good morning Freedom family and a special welcome to our visitors. My name is Pastor Jake Littlefield, and today, I want to talk to you about forgiveness."

Amens were heard throughout the sanctuary.

"Forgiveness must come before healing." He continued. "Some of you are hurting from the pains of your past. People you trusted, let you down. They broke your heart. You are battling with questions of why. You are tossing and turning at night. Peace seems so far away, but today, I have come to let you know that forgiveness is the gateway to your healing, joy, and peace."

The preacher's words became faint as Bethany thought about the people she needed to forgive. But they never admitted nor apologized for their wrongdoings, she started to think before she heard the preacher's final words.

"Forgiveness doesn't need permission. Some people will never ask for it, but that doesn't mean you can't still forgive. Forgiveness is really about giving yourself permission to be free from the hurt, pain, and the disappointment that affected you."

Bethany pondered the preacher's words the rest of the day. She thought about when Caleb failed to mention that he was legally married after several weeks of dating him, and how he had reneged on his promise to help her move by paying for the U-Haul. Twice!

She thought about how she would have never moved to Newnan if she knew they weren't going to be together. Her heart began to race as she thought about the day he told her that he proposed to Kacey five months before their last reconnection. He never mentioned that to her until after she moved. The proposal to Kacey sent her over the edge, and it took a wing and prayer to bring her back. Even with all that Caleb did she always gave him another chance, because he said he loved her and that she was the woman God created for him.

Still pondering the painful thoughts of the past and the preacher's words, she pulled out her journal from her nightstand and grabbed a pen just before going to bed.

> *Forgiveness, I don't understand you at all, but I have learned that you are the gateway to the healing for my soul. So, I choose to forgive. I forgive Nick. I forgive Caleb. I forgive Roman. I forgive God. Lastly, I forgive me. I don't want the hurt, the shame, and the disappointments anymore. I want real love instead.*

Bethany closed her book and slept better that night than she had in three months.

"Hey, Beth. You sound better this morning."

Bethany could not wait for her morning talk with Ne'cole to tell her about her experience at church.

"Hey, Necy. How are you?"

"This question is how are you. Spill it."

"What are you talking about lady?"

"Don't play with me. You sound happy. Who is it?"

"Jesus."

They both laughed.

"Nikki, church, was amazing yesterday and I let a lot of things go."

"Oh really."

"Yeah, girl and I slept so good, and I feel more energized."

"That's what I wanted to hear."

"Plus, I guess a little eye candy didn't hurt either."

"Who!?"

"I don't know his name, but that butterscotch hunk who sat next to me yesterday at church. Girl, I had to fight to stay focus."

"Honey, there isn't anything wrong with a little eye candy. Who knows he might have been checking you out too."

"Nikki, I wasn't concerned with him at all. I stayed focus on the word and got what I really needed."

"Butterscotch had something you needed too."

"Bye, Necy. Have a great day."

"Bye. Love you girl."

Her notification sound interrupted the sounds of Jill Scott's song Golden through her car speakers shortly after her call with Ne'cole. She pressed the read text message button on the navigation screen. A rubber smell filled the air as she slammed on the brakes after seeing the message was from Caleb. "What in the hell does he want? I know I blocked his number!" She quickly remembered she no longer had her android phone and couldn't convert her data to her new phone. Thank goodness she stopped in enough time from hitting the car that was braking to make a right turn. She pulled over to collect her nerves and to see what he had to say five months after their break up.

Hey Bethany. I hope you are doing well. You have been on my mind a lot, and I was wondering if we can meet up to talk. I will be on your side of town a few days this week for work.

"Oh, Hell Naw, Hell to the Naw," Bethany uttered in disbelief. "I can't believe this."

"Call Ne'cole." She spoke after she pressed the voice command button.

"Answer the phone Nikki," Bethany anxiously said after three rings.

"You have reached the…" Bethany hung up the phone and called her again.

"Come on Nikki. Pickup." Desperation filled Bethany's chest as she needed her bestie on this, but she reached her voicemail again.

Bethany released a heavy sigh and decided not to respond to his text immediately. She had some praying to do and by praying she mostly meant talking to Nikki.

Totally distracted, Bethany didn't accomplish much at work, but her mind stayed busy. She decided to leave work a little early to take a nap and maybe her mind would finally find rest. Before she did, she glanced at Caleb's text once again and texted her response.

Hello, Caleb. I am great. I hope the thoughts were good. Can we not speak over the phone?

Almost immediately Caleb texted back.

Bethany! I am so glad you returned my text. Of course, they were good thoughts. You have been nothing but good to me. I would rather speak face to face. I only need about thirty minutes of your time.

Bethany deeply inhaled and flopped on the bed to exhale. *What the heck? Actually, it would be nice to see him too.* She secretly thought to herself.

I can meet you tomorrow.

***

Great! How about the Barnes and Nobles off Newnan Crossing at 7 pm?

***

That works.

***

127

Okay, see you then.

Bethany laid down for her nap, but as soon as her head hit the pillow, she was awakened by another call.

"Nikki!"

"Hey, Girlie. I have been in meetings all day. Sorry, I am just now calling you back. What's going on?"

"Girl, you won't believe who I heard from this morning."

"Who? Butterscotch!"

Bethany's anxiousness momentarily ceased to laugh at the serious yet comical guess.

"No! Caleb! He wants to meet to talk face to face."

"You are lying. When?"

"Tomorrow."

"Are you going?"

"I…I know I shouldn't, after all, he has put me through, but I told him yes."

"What does he want to talk about?"

"Girl, your guess is better than mine. I have no earthly idea."

"Bethany?…"

"Yes."

"Bethany, I love you so much, and you are like my sister. But I haven't always told you the truth, because I don't want to lose your friendship."

"What are you talking about Nikki?"

"I don't think Caleb is the one for you. I know you love him, but his love is controlling and manipulative. You deserve so much better than that. You gotta let him go. Don't give him any more of your time or energy."

"I'm not like you Nikki. I just can't kick people out of my life. Caleb and I were friends for almost five years."

"Do you really consider him a friend after what he did to you?"

"At some point, I believe what we had was real."

"Just be careful Bethany. Don't let him get you back so easily."

"I just need to see what this is about Nikki. Then I can finally be done with all of this."

"Well, I want to know all the details."

"You know you will girl."

After her conversation with Ne'cole, Bethany felt like she had made a mistake by agreeing to meet Caleb. But what if he wants to admit his wrong and ask for forgiveness, what if he has broken up with his fiancée, or what if God convicted him and he wants me now. The "ifs" continued to linger in her mind as she tried to fall asleep, but sleep wouldn't come. So, Bethany decided to go down to the local neighborhood market to pick up items for her lunch the next day.

"Excuse me."

Bethany looked over her left shoulder as she was placing a loaf of bread in her basket. She stood in awe as she looked at her Jonathon from Sunday's service at Freedom.

"Excuse me. I don't mean to interrupt your shopping, but I recognized you from church, and I wanted to speak to you."

"Yes, we sat by each other at the noon service. My name is Bethany."

"Bethany! That is the place where Jesus performed a lot of His miracles."

Bethany smiled. Most people don't have that knowledge or make that connection. "Yes, it is, and your name is...?"

"Forgive me. My name is Asa."

"Are you a doctor Asa?"

"No, why do you ask?"

"Because your name means healer," Bethany flirtatiously said.

"Interesting, most people don't know the meaning of my name."

"Well, I am not most people."

They both laughed.

"Are you a Freedom Chapel member, I haven't seen you there before."

"I have visited twice, but I'm not a member. I recently moved here from Huntsville."

"Huntsville, AL?"

"Yes."

"I graduated from Albert Lee Magnet High School."

"No way."

"Yes, I moved to Atlanta when I started at Morehouse, and I just decided to stay here for work."

"That's cool. I went to UAB."

"Go Blazers, huh?"

"That's right."

"What brought you here?"

"It's a long story, but I am hoping to branch out more with my writing here."

"That's where I've seen you before. You're Bethany, the author of Love's Lottery."

"Yeah, that's me."

"I saw you in the Metro-Atlanta Herald."

"Yeah, I cut my hair shortly after that picture was taken."

"You still look amazing."

"Well, thank you, kind sir."

"Look. The church is hosting a singles' meetup at the church tomorrow, and I would love for you to come."

"Sure, what time?"

"Seven."

"Cool. I don't think I have plans. I'd love to come."

"Great! Here is my card. If you need anything while getting acclimated to the city or the church or if you just want to talk, give me a call."

"Thank you so much. You can have my card too."

"Great running into you Bethany, and I will see you tomorrow."

"Yes, thanks for the invite. I will see you tomorrow."

While putting her groceries away and preparing her lunch, she heard her phone ringing in her purse. Running to catch the call, she didn't recognize the number but answered it anyway.

"Hello?"

"Hello, Bethany. This is Asa."

"Oh, hi Asa. I didn't have your number saved yet."

"It's quite alright. I just wanted to check to see if you made it in safely."

"Awe, thank you, Asa. I did. I was fixing my lunch for tomorrow."

"What are you taking?"

"Just a chicken salad sandwich and some fruit."

"Sounds good."

"Yeah, I'm trying to eat healthier these days."

"I need to do the same." He laughed. "So, Bethany. I apologize if my direct approach offends you, but I am interested in getting to know you."

"No offense taken."

"I noticed you on Sunday, and your worship was attractive to me not to mention your natural beauty. You seemed solely focused on the Word, and I didn't want to distract you. I asked God for another opportunity to see you. I told Him, I wouldn't let the next opportunity pass without speaking to you. When I saw you at the store, I swallowed every fear and approached you."

"Asa, I really appreciate your direct approach and honesty. I must admit that you had my attention for a moment at church."

"Just a moment?"

They both laughed.

"Actually, I was trying to stay focused. I needed that word that Pastor Jake taught on forgiveness."

"Yeah, I think we all needed that Word. So, let me ask you because I don't want to be disrespectful. I didn't see a ring, but are you single?"

"I am. Are you?"

"Yes, I am single indeed."

"Single Indeed?"

"Yes, I have no girlfriend or friends with benefits."

"I see. That is great. I guess I am single indeed too."

Bethany and Asa talked for three hours that night. It had been so refreshing for her to have conversations with a man that seemed to have connected with her on so many levels. Too tired to do anything after getting off the phone with Asa, Bethany fell fast asleep.

The alarm notification startled Bethany as she reached for her phone to snooze it. The clock read six-forty-five. She jumped out of bed into the shower. While drying herself off, a text notification came from her phone. She walked over to the bed and picked up the phone. Bethany pressed the message icon to see who it was.

Good morning, Beautiful. Words cannot express how running into you yesterday made my day. I pray that you have a day full of miracles and blessings. I can't wait to see you at the meetup tonight. Asa.

Bethany turned and sat on the bed holding the phone to her chest as if the phone was Asa himself. She felt peace deep within. Something she had not known for over a year. They seemed to fit like a glove, but Bethany knew it was too early to tell so, she worked to play it cool. She was determined to not make the same mistake with Asa as she did with Roman. She questioned, *Am I moving too fast without asking the important questions or should I just go along with the flow?* She thought about her book tips..."not being too available and going on ten dates before committing to a relationship," but all of that seemed to go out the window with Asa. She really enjoyed their conversation.

Her snooze alarm sounded in her hand. Bethany looked at the phone. "Seven o'clock. I got to be out the door in forty-five minutes," she verbally thought. Bethany tapped the keypad and quickly replied to his text.

Good morning, Asa. You are too kind. I am looking forward to seeing you too. Have a blessed day.

She continued to sit and take in the moment until she heard another notification. She thought it was Asa saying have a blessed day too, so she waited to open it after she finished getting dressed and got to the car.

"No!" Bethany screamed. "I totally forgot."

Bethany stared at the text message from earlier.

Good morning, Sexy. I can't wait to see you tonight at Barnes and Nobles.

Asa had taken her mind off of Caleb, and the fact that she agreed to meet him. It slipped her mind that it was the same time as the meetup.

Delaying her response, Bethany prayed all day for direction. Caleb had been the love of her life for over four years. No matter how much she tried to date and move on, Caleb always had her heart. Bethany aguishly cried because deep down she still had hope for that magical day when they would become husband and wife, but she was tired of the merry-go-rounds with love. She wanted to do the right thing, but her right always seemed to be wrong. She desperately wanted to talk things over with Ne'cole, but she already knew what she would say. Ne'cole hated Caleb. So, she turned to the only person who was omniscient and omnipresent and could really lead her to the right path.

Immediately coming in from work, Bethany ran into her room and fell on her knees beside her bed. She wept like a newborn baby for what seemed like an eternity before she uttered her prayer to the Lord.

"Dear God, I want to thank You for never leaving me through the good times or bad times in my life. I have made a lot of mistakes when it comes to love. I have even blamed you for some of my mistakes. I feel like I keep repeating cycles in my love affairs and I am tired. I was really moving on, and now, my recycled love has come for me. I told him that I would meet him today because he wanted to talk face to face. I completely forgot after meeting Asa at the store. I don't know what to do. I do love Caleb. I'm just tired of his immaturity. I need you to guide my footsteps and show me the path I should take. Is Caleb your will for me?"

Bethany ended her prayer and started to get dressed. Foundation was her friend today as she powdered her face and concealed and highlighted her eyes. She pulled out her new fuchsia lipstick from Mac and added the finishing touch to her look. She still didn't know what she was going to do, but she did expect for God to answer her prayer.

As she approached the main highway, she contemplated whether to turn left which would take her to Caleb or right which would take her to the church. Her thoughts were interrupted with a loud honk from the car behind her and Bethany hastily made a quick left.

Seven minutes later, Bethany pulled up to Barnes and Nobles and parked the car. *Could my dreams of being with Caleb be coming true?* Bethany started to envision the finale of her nearly fifth year "off and on" relationship with Caleb. She saw them both pouring out the "I'm sorry" followed by the passionate kiss as if the minister said you may now kiss the bride. She accepted the thoughts that her days as a single woman was over. The dreadful online dating was over. The "start and stop again" process of the dating hassle was over. Sex without guilt was over. It was worth it all having the love of her life connected with her now and forever.

Her eyes perused the store from the car to see if she saw Caleb inside. No Caleb. She looked around the parking lot to see if she could spot his car, but her search was interrupted by a loud bing sound from her phone. She looked down to see it was a text message from Caleb.

Hey. I'm in the café. Have you made it yet?

***

Be there in a sec. Bethany replied after she spot checked to make sure her eyes and nose were still clean. She smiled to make sure nothing was in her teeth. Finally, she popped a mint in her mouth and opened the car door.

"Wow!" Caleb stood with both his eyes and mouth wide open.

"Are you just going to stand there?" Bethany smiled as if she didn't know she was looking breathtaking.

"Beth-a-ny. Baby, you are amazingly beautiful. I love your haircut."

"Thank you Caleb." She pleasantly smiled.

"So, can I get a hug?"

"Of course." Bethany walked closer to embrace him. They hugged for a split second before taking a seat near the windows in the café.

"Bethany. Thank you for meeting me here tonight. I really needed to get some things off my chest."

"I'm all ears." Bethany sat all composed, but internally she was quite the opposite.

138

"Well, first I want to say how proud I am of you."

"For what?" She inquisitively asked.

"For the book and the great things coming along with that. I remember us sitting my couch back in Huntsville. You would lay your feet on my legs. I would massage them as you talked about your dreams of being an author."

"I remember that." Bethany chimed in. "I enjoyed those times together."

"Me too."

Fighting the urge to just tell him to get to the point, Bethany continued to sit patiently, as he took the scenic route to the real reason they were meeting.

Caleb sat staring at Bethany's beautiful transformation while Bethany's patience had run its course.

"Why are we here, Caleb?"

"I miss you."

"Are you still with Kacey?"

Caleb sat quietly with his hands over his face and let out a deep breath.

Caleb was not quite ready to get on the subject of Kacey, but surprisingly, Bethany had become a straight shooter. He wasn't ready for that as he was still trying to have his cake and eat it too. He didn't love Kacey like he loved Bethany, but Kacey never left him during his financial troubles, sickness, and even his infidelity with Bethany. She was his ride or die chic or a fool in love as Bethany called her. Caleb sat quietly struggling within himself, trying to think of justifiable reasons for wanting to see Bethany.

Bethany noticed the ring tan on his wedding finger. She refused to play this game with Caleb again and answered her own question for him by excusing herself from the table as she congratulated him.

Bethany felt empowered as God must have prepared her heart because she did not cry a single tear. It actually inspired her to wait on God's best, as she rebuked the thought that bombarded her mind that Caleb won because he got a spouse.

As she walked out the door, she never looked back or even wondered about his reaction. At that moment she realized that character trumps coincidence. In the past, she dismissed so many of Caleb's character flaws, because of the many situations that kept bringing them into each other's life. But not anymore, she saw clear through him as if he was made of crystal glass, and enough was enough.

Bethany was tired of retaking the life test with men, and to receive the best she would have to pass. Unlike what she witnessed in the public schools, she knew God didn't socially promote. She had to learn the necessary lessons to receive what her heart truly desired. She wanted blessings that added no sorrow, and she left sorrow sitting at the table.

Making it to church during the first worship song, Bethany went straight to the altar and got on her knees. She greatly appreciated Asa's invitation and realized he was a part of her journey of reconnecting with her Maker and discovering the purpose for her pain. She wasn't quite ready to enter a new relationship, as she was beginning to cultivate a relationship with herself. As she got ready for bed after such an eventful evening, Bethany looked at herself in the mirror. She reminded herself that even though she didn't get who she thought was her knight in shining armor she obtained something far greater. Self-Love.

About the Author

SANDREKA WAS BORN AND raised in Chambers County, Alabama with two incredible parents, one sibling, and a host of supportive family and friends. She is a graduate of the University of Alabama at Birmingham, LaGrange College, and Jacksonville State University. She draws upon her interest of religion, life, and relationships to fuel her creative writing. Sandreka is a national board certified mathematics teacher who also enjoys writing. In 2015, she became a published author with her teacher devotionals. She transitioned to writing fiction short stories, and she released her first story, *Recycled Love* in March 2017. *Love Bethany* is her sixth publication and her first novel.